off limits

SONS OF THE UNDERGROUND BOOK 1

WALL STREET JOURNAL & USA TODAY BEST SELLING AUTHOR

TERRI ANNE BROWNING

Off-Limits
Sons of the Underground Book 1
Written by Terri Anne Browning

Cover Design Cassy Roop of Pink Ink Designs
Edited by Lisa Hollett of Silently Correcting Your Grammar
Formatting by M.L. Pahl of IndieVention Designs

ISBN: 9781697415674

10 9 8 7 6 5 4 3 2 1

off limits

SONS OF THE UNDERGROUND BOOK 1

prologue

Howler

"Chin down, but don't break eye contact. Always know where your enemy is," I instructed, showing her the stance she needed to stay in.

Her dark gaze was focused on Downtown, the "threat" I was training her against today. Not that Lyla Bennet needed me to train her. Between her brother and her cousin Barrick, she'd been taught how to fight from the time she could walk.

No, this was for me. To keep me from losing my mind when she wasn't an arm's length away. Which was ninety percent of the time, meaning I was constantly worried about her safety. If I couldn't have her for myself, I at least needed to know she would be okay when I wasn't near her.

Downtown kept his eyes trained on Lyla, making sure not to break eye contact, but I saw him shudder and knew he was scared shitless. Whether it was fear of the girl in front of him about to bring the pain, or me and the ass-kicking I would give him in a heartbeat if he hurt her, I wasn't sure.

Either way, he needed to be scared. Because whether it was Lyla or me, Downtown was about to get his ass beat.

"You're boring me, Downtown," Lyla sassed, a smirk on her beautiful face. "We doing this or not?"

For half a second, his eyes drifted to me, and I knew then he was more scared of me than her. As he should be. Because I would annihilate him if he harmed her, even if it was by accident.

"Come on, pussy," she snapped when he didn't move, causing him to flinch and his face to turn red with both embarrassment and anger. "What? Are you scared of a little bitty girl? You should be. I'll kick your ass and make you cry for your mommy. Boo-fucking-hoo. Downtown got dropped on his head by a girl. Bet they won't ever let you in the cage again because you can't even handle me, let alone another Son of the Underground."

With a growl full of rage, he charged her. She laughed, an evil, sexy sound that went straight to my cock, which instantly made me feel like a bastard. Lyla was only seventeen. Her birthday was just a few weeks away, but it still made me feel like a dirty creep for wanting her as badly as I did. I was used to that feeling, though. I'd been feeling it for a hell of a lot longer than I ever should have where this girl was concerned, but no matter what I did, I couldn't stop it.

In Downtown's blind anger, he didn't see the way she moved, and in the next moment, he was lying on his back on the mat, the air knocked out of his lungs. The sound he made as he tried to gasp for air was disturbing, but she crouched down beside him. "Remember this the next time I hear you talking shit about me being at the Underground. Because I will drop your ass in front of everyone if you ever say that about me again. Clear?" She gave him a little grin, patted him on the top of his dreadlocked head, and straightened.

"What the fuck did he say about you?" I demanded as I followed her over to the bench where her gym bag and water bottle were.

She lifted the bottle and took a thirty swallow. With a shrug, she sat on the bench beside her bag and grabbed her phone. "Not important. If he's smart, he won't ever say it again."

"If you tell me what he said, I'll make sure he never speaks again," I promised, sitting beside her.

Lyla turned so she was half facing me, her bare knee brushing against my thigh. My cock jumped at the contact, but her eyes were on mine and thankfully not on my lap. "I don't need you to fight my battles, Howler. Nor do I need your protection. I'm not fragile."

I rubbed my hand over my mouth, itching to just grab her and kiss her until she realized why I wanted—fucking needed—to protect her. "I don't want to protect you because you're fragile," I whisper-growled at her, making her eyes darken. I clenched my hands into fists to keep from reaching for her. "I *need* to protect you because you are precious to me, Lyla."

"Howler…" she breathed, but I got to my feet and walked away before I did something stupid that I couldn't take back.

"I have to go. Picking Josie up from my mom's, and if I'm late, she'll bitch at me." I threw up a hand, waving as I walked away.

Even as my soul bellowed at me to go back and get that girl and take her with me.

***

Pulling up in front of the three-story house, I gritted my teeth. I didn't want to come tonight, but Judge said it was important. When my best friend said he needed me to do something, I tried not to let him down.

Judge was there for me when I needed him the most. Right after my dad died, leaving me in charge of my mother and sisters, along with his company, my ex told me she was pregnant. If it weren't for my best friend, I would have lost my mind and maybe the construction company my father had spent his life building from the bottom up.

I owed him my loyalty because he'd always had my back. But my feelings for Lyla constantly kept me at odds with myself. I wanted her so fucking badly, but I knew I'd never get to call her mine because of Judge. He'd made it clear years ago if anyone so much as touched his sister, they would lose his respect, his friendship, and any chance of being a part of the Underground ever again.

Stepping out of my SUV, I opened the back door and reached for the baby's car seat. Josie was sound asleep, so I grabbed the diaper bag and walked up the steps to Judge's house. Before I could ring the doorbell, the door swung open and the housekeeper smiled fondly up at me.

"Hello, Mr. Bronson."

"Mabel," I greeted.

"Everyone is in the family room," she informed me, eyeballing the car seat longingly. Ever since Josie was born a year ago, everyone who saw her fell in love with my daughter. Myself included.

When her mother told me she was pregnant, my first thought was to pay for an abortion. Gwen wanted one, and at the time, I was more than happy to pay the exorbitant amount of cash to get her and the baby out of my life.

Then my mother found out and stepped in. She moved Gwen in to her house, made sure she stayed healthy throughout the entire pregnancy, and forced me to be in the delivery room when Josie came into the world.

I was thankful my mom did all that. Because the instant my baby girl was placed in my arms, I knew what love at first sight was. She ruined me, destroying any and all reservations I had about being a single father.

There was no way in hell I was letting my psycho ex have full custody, and because I had friends like Judge, I'd been awarded primary custody, while Gwen was only given a few days a week with our little girl.

I knew it made me look like a bastard, keeping a mother away from her baby, but I also knew in my heart Josie was better off with me the majority of the time than when Gwen. I didn't regret taking Gwen to court, and I didn't feel a lick of guilt for pulling out the big guns with my connections to ensure Josie remained with me. I would do it all over again. Fuck, I would do worse, if that was what it came to, just to keep my precious little baby with me.

Nodding at Mabel, I carried Josie down the hall to the family room. The house was huge, much too big for Judge and Lyla alone. But Lyla loved this house, so Judge had never even talked about moving after their father died. As I walked in, I saw Judge and his sister sitting on the couch in front of the fireplace, their heads bent together as they spoke to each other in hushed whispers. My eyes lingered on Lyla, who looked pissed at her brother as she shook her head adamantly at him.

"Howler," a voice I wasn't expecting called out.

Turning my head, I found Barrick walking toward me. Known as Beast in the Underground cages, Lyla and Judge's cousin looked exactly like he was some kind of good-looking beast from a fairy tale, with his long mahogany hair, thick beard, and dark eyes. The female population went crazy for him in and out of the cage, and all of his groupies always wore *Beauty and the Beast*-themed shirts whenever he had a fight.

Lyla was beside me before her cousin could get halfway across the room to shake my hand. But it wasn't me she was excited to see. Instead, she pulled the car seat from my hands and placed it on the floor. Crouching down, she unclipped the straps and pulled Josie easily from the seat without waking her.

My eyes were glued to Lyla's every move, still amazed even after seeing her do that a hundred times, that she could so effortlessly handle my daughter without disturbing her sleep. I'd never been able to accomplish that maneuver and doubted I ever would.

It took everything in me not to gather them both in my arms and just hide. I wanted to say to hell with everything and everyone else, and just keep Josie and Lyla locked in my house away from the world, have a stolen little piece of paradise for myself.

Straightening, Lyla cupped the back of Josie's head and placed her against her shoulder, still without waking the baby. "Hello, sweet Jo-Jo," she murmured softly.

Josie yawned loudly then opened her eyes and smiled right at Lyla. With her chubby little hand, she tried to grab at Lyla's long dark hair. Laughing, Lyla easily evaded the little grasp, kissing the baby's hand instead and getting a giggle as her reward.

"There's my girl," Lyla cooed. "What have you been doing, Jo-Jo? Has Daddy been taking good care of you?"

Josie started jabbering and gurgling, and Lyla pretended like they were having a full conversation.

It always hurt me to watch them together. Josie never smiled as big for anyone as she did with Lyla. And Lyla always lit up the brightest when Josie was in her arms. I ached to make us a family, to give in and say to hell with everything else, but Judge's friendship was too important to me.

"See?" Judge grumbled as he walked over to stand beside his sister, but even though his tone was anything but happy, he still smiled at his goddaughter. "Won't you miss this if you go?"

I zeroed in on that immediately, and for some reason, I felt a flash of panic hit me hard. "Go? Go where?"

Lyla turned away without meeting my gaze and walked over to the couch to sit with Josie in her lap. I focused on Judge instead. "Go where?" I gritted out.

Barrick cleared his throat. "I need a partner in a new job I'm doing for my stepfather. Lyla is going to help me."

"Help you on a job?" I shook my head. "No. She's only seventeen. She can't be helping you on a security job. No way."

"She's going to be eighteen in less than a month," her cousin reminded me. "And yes, she can. Lyla wanted the job. I've already gotten it sorted with my stepdad, and Aunt Brenda gave her permission."

"Where is it?" I asked, glaring at the man who wanted to take Lyla away from me.

"California," he answered with a casual shrug. "Look, it's nothing dangerous. She's just going to help me keep an eye on a spoiled little college girl for a few months. I'm not taking her to some war-torn country or having her go undercover with the cartel. Jesus, relax. Both of you."

"But she's only seventeen," I muttered, rubbing my hand across my mouth.

"So you keep reminding me," she said with a grunt, then smiled down at Josie. "Daddy is never going to let me forget that, is he, Jo-Jo?"

"I don't like it," I told Barrick, taking a menacing step in his direction.

Barrick only smirked, ready to take me on, but it was Judge's voice that kept me from putting my fist through the other fighter's pretty face. "Howler, rules," he said, but his tone was laced with frustration, as if he wanted to punch his cousin just as much as I did.

But he was right. There were rules. No fighting outside the Underground.

That was just one of many rules Judge had for the Sons who fought in his cages. Fighting anywhere else was the quickest way to get you kicked out of the Underground. The second was trying anything with Lyla. From the moment she grew tits, Judge had set that rule in stone. No one was allowed to date his sister. Fuck, they weren't even allowed to think about her.

I'd done plenty of thinking and fantasizing, not that I would ever admit it out loud. But touching her, making her mine, wasn't possible. It would mean choosing between her and Judge—and the Underground. As long as I kept myself in check, I wouldn't lose anything.

But if I gave in, I could lose everything.

Including my best friend.

"Let's grab a bottle of wine to go with dinner," Judge suggested, already walking out of the room.

Following him, I stomped down the hall to the door that led into the wine cellar, knowing this was why he'd asked me to come tonight. This was what was so important.

Lyla was going to leave, and he wanted me to know.

We were both quiet until we got to the bottom of the stairs. Then my friend turned, a look of misery on his face. “Talk to her,” he ordered. “Tell her not to go. Convince her Josie needs her to stay close. Anything. I don’t care at this point. Whatever you have to do, just get her to stay.”

I gave him a long appraisal, seeing the desperation in his dark eyes. A desperate Judge was an unpredictable Judge, and that was dangerous. His sister, however, was his lifeline. If I were honest with myself, she was mine too. But for Judge, it was completely different. For so long, it had just been him and Lyla. After his bastard of a father died, their mother went MIA, spending more time with her boyfriends—who were younger than her son—than her children. Judge was left to raise Lyla on his own because of it, which made Brenda Bennet giving her permission for this job seem laughable.

“You realize we’re talking about Lyla, right?” I reminded him. “She’s so damn stubborn, Judge. If she has her mind set on this, nothing will dissuade her. Especially not me.”

“Well, figure something out. I want my sister to stay here, not go to fuck-knows-where with Barrick. Look, I trust him with her, I do. But he can’t predict what she will do if she gets in one of her moods. You can. Just…do something, Howler.”

I knew what I wanted to do to convince her to stay, but Judge would kill me if I did it.

Fuck.

“I’ll do my best,” I assured him, not the least bit confident that I could accomplish this task he’d given me.

***

“Don’t even say it,” Lyla growled in a quiet voice as she placed Josie in her car seat and fastened her in.

“I didn’t even open my mouth.” Crossing my arms over my chest, I watched her with my baby daughter, wishing more than anything she were Josie’s mother instead of Gwen.

Once Josie was secured, Lyla stood and placed her hands on her narrow hips. “You didn’t have to. I know you too well, Graham Bronson.” I flinched at her using my real name. "Judge told you to talk me out of going with Barrick, didn't he?"

"No comment," I muttered, glancing around the family room. Barrick had left, and Judge had gone to his den to return some phone calls in an attempt to give me a chance to talk to Lyla.

Her mouth tilted up on one side, and she shook her head at me. "It's cute that you're both so worried about me, but I'm a big girl now, Howler. I can take care of myself."

"I know that," I grumbled. "But maybe I want to take care of you anyway."

She inhaled sharply, her eyes lighting up as she stepped closer to me. "Then you know what I want." Her hand flattened against the center of my chest, and she looked up at me through her thick, dark lashes. "I will let you take care of me, Howler. I'll even stay here with you and Josie. All it's going to take is for you to say the words and give me what I want the most."

My heart thudded loudly in my ears. Clenching my eyes closed, I covered her hand, pressing it harder against my chest and savoring her touch. Three words, that was all it would take, all I would have to utter and she would be mine.

She would stay, and Judge would be happy. We all would.

But those three words would change everything.

Making her mine would get me kicked out of the Underground.

I would lose Judge.

I'd already lost so much; I wasn't ready to lose either of those. Not now. Not ever.

Opening my eyes, I told her the truth, even though a part of me died inside as the words left my mouth. "I can't, Lyla."

The hope that had been shining out of her eyes only seconds before burned to ash right in front of me. Jerking her hand out of mine, she stepped back, and it took a willpower I didn't realize I possessed to keep from pulling her back to me. "You should go. I have some packing to do. I'm leaving in the morning."

"Lyla, don't go," I tried. But she shook her head and put more distance between us, while I scrambled to find a reason to keep her from leaving. "Please… Josie. She loves you. She needs you."

I love you.

I need you.

Don't leave us.

Yet I kept the words I knew would hold her to me from spilling out.

Her gaze fell on the sleeping baby in her car seat and lingered, longing pouring from her. "I love Josie. I would do anything for her. But if I stayed, I'd only be giving you permission to break my heart over and over again. Like you do every damn day I see you and you continue to pretend like you don't want the same things I do."

"It isn't that I don't want them, baby," I confessed. "It's that I can't have any of them."

"No, Graham. You can have anything you want. You just don't have the balls to fight for it." A tear fell from her eyes, breaking me, but before I could reach for her, she turned away. "You should go. Jo-Jo should be in her crib at home, enjoying the slumber of the innocent."

"Lyla—"

"Goodbye, Howler."

"Lyla!" I barked, only to startle Josie awake. She began to cry just as Lyla's shoulder began to shake, and I knew Lyla was silently doing the same as my baby girl, but she didn't pause.

She walked out of the room with her head held high, leaving me standing there helplessly, watching her go and fighting my own tears.

one

Lyla

THREE YEARS LATER

I hit the sidewalk running, my heart already pounding so hard I could barely breathe.

My roommate's call just moments before had equal doses of rage and fear burning through me, making the workout I'd just finished with my cousin Braxton seem like a leisurely stroll through the park in comparison.

Something was wrong with Josie. Mia said she'd seen bruises on her and suspected there were more that Josie wouldn't let her see.

I knew in my heart, all the way to the depths of my soul, that it wasn't Howler who'd put those marks on his daughter.

It was Gwen. It had to be her. That selfish cow only thought about herself. Josie deserved a better mother than the one she'd been birthed to.

And I'd always wished I was the one to fill that position, but stupid Howler was too much of a pussy.

I got to the dance school in record time, but I stood outside for a few minutes, trying to get my breathing and my emotions under control. Instinct was screaming for me to just run in there, scoop up Josie, and never let her go, but I couldn't do that in my current condition without scaring her.

Once my heart rate had slowed a little and I could actually breathe again, I wiped the sweat off my face with the bottom of my shirt and walked as calmly as I could into the studio.

The place was quiet except for the music coming from a classroom down the hall. Mia's second class of the evening was the last class on Tuesdays, so there was no one left in the building but her and her students. I forced myself to walk and not run, but as soon as I pushed open the door and saw Josie, I lost it.

"Lyla!" Josie exclaimed, running toward me excitedly.

I hadn't seen her in a few days, but apparently that was enough time for her fucking mother to hurt my girl and make her scared to talk about it.

She jumped into my arms, and I held her close, breathing in her clean, baby-shampoo smell. I clenched my eyes closed for a moment.

“Did you come to pick me up?” she asked hopefully, tipping her head back to look at me.

“I’m never letting you out of my sight again,” I vowed, kissing her forehead and inhaling deeply again. Having her in my arms and being able to smell her little girl scent calmed me and kept me from wanting to do something I knew I shouldn’t.

Like finding Gwen and stomping her ass into the ground before I put a bullet between her eyes.

“Really? You promise?”

Something in her eyes and the way she so skeptically asked me to promise broke my heart, and I blinked back tears. “Pinkie promise,” I choked out.

She wrapped her finger around mine, and we touched our thumbs together, sealing the promise just as the door slammed open, making the other little girls in the class yelp in fright. Out of the corner of my eye, I saw Mia put herself in front of the raging bull storming toward us.

“Daddy.” Josie clung to my neck, but she smiled up at her father. “Are you picking me up too?”

"Yes, baby girl." His eyes were wild, but he couldn't seem to control himself. "Let me have her, Lyla."

"No way." I tightened my hold on her, shaking my head. "I have her now, and I'm not ever letting her go again."

That got me a beaming smile from Josie but a growl from Howler. He took a step closer, trying to intimidate me into giving him what he wanted, but I stood my ground. I would fight him then and there if he tried to pull her out of my arms by force. In my heart, Josie was my baby just as much as she was his, and I would protect her with my last breath.

The door swung open again, and I wasn't surprised to see my cousin Barrick run in, sweat dripping off him. Braxton must have called him, but I hadn't told Brax anything other than to call Howler and tell him to meet me at Josie's dance school.

Barrick was in over his head with Mia—hell, we all were where she was concerned—but my older cousin was drowning this time around. I'd never seen him care so much about a job. I felt guilty for my part in deceiving Mia, as did Braxton, but neither of our guilt could compare to Barrick's. He was trying his hardest to get out of this job so he wouldn't lose Mia if she ever found out what was going on.

Howler touched Josie's back, making her flinch. I felt more than saw it, and I tuned out everything but Josie. "Did that hurt?" I asked her quietly, and after a small hesitation, she buried her face in my neck and nodded.

I didn't even hear Mia and Barrick taking the other kids out of the room, but when I placed Josie on her feet, it was to find that everyone else was gone. Dropping to my knees in front of Josie, I gently cupped her sweet, angelic little face in my hands.

"Jo-Jo, what happened to make your back hurt?"

"N-nothing," she stuttered. "I-I fell."

"Did your mommy tell you to say that?" I asked in a soft, quiet voice so I wouldn't scare her, when on the inside, a storm was starting to rage out of control.

There was another hesitation, but she finally nodded as two fat tears fell from her eyes.

"Can I see your back?"

"No!" Josie backed up a few steps, shaking her head so hard her hair started to fall from the ponytail it was in. "No, you and Daddy will get mad at me. Mommy said if I let anyone see Daddy won't want to see me anymore. He… He w-won't l-love me anymore." More tears fell, and I had to put a hand to my throat, willing my heart to stay in my chest.

"Josie." Howler's voice was gentle, belying the rage blazing from his eyes. "Nothing, and I mean nothing, will ever keep me from wanting to see you. I love you more than anything. That won't ever change, sweetheart. I promise you."

"But Mommy said," she cried. "She said you will be mad at me. I don't want you to be mad at me, Daddy."

"I'm not mad, baby girl. I swear to you. Lyla isn't mad either. Are you, Lyla?" He fell to his knees beside me, making the two of us seem like a united front. In that moment, we were.

"Right. I'd never get mad at you, Jo-Jo. You're my best friend in the world. Remember? We can tell each other anything." I held out my hands, silently begging her to put her hand in mine. "Please, Jo. Tell me what happened."

"Y-you promise you won't get m-mad?" she whispered.

I held up my pinkie to her. "I promise."

She wrapped her little finger around mine then touched her thumb to my own. "I-I spilled juice on my new outfit. I didn't mean to, I swear. But…but it was grape juice, and Mommy said my outfit was expensive. She grabbed me, and she shook me. My teeth snapped together, and I bit my tongue. When I spit…" She let out a shuddery little breath. "When I spit out the blood, it got on her new outfit too, and she hit me." She touched her back with her hands. "She hit me a lot. It hurt, Lyla. I-it still hurts."

I felt Howler begin to shake, and with my free hand, I touched his back. His entire body seemed to jolt at the contact, but he didn't move away. Instead, he leaned into my touch, and within seconds, his shaking subsided.

"Will you show me, Jo-Jo?" I asked, still trying to keep my voice calm.

"O-okay." She finally gave in, and I was glad. I didn't want to force her, but I feared that was what it would have come to.

She turned her back to me and slowly started to lower her leotard. I got to my feet to help her. When she revealed the dark, painful-looking bruises on her lower back, I had to bite back a gasp. Howler's gaze caught mine, and what I was feeling was reflected in his eyes.

"What did she hit you with, Josie?" her father asked gruffly.

"One of my toys," she mumbled.

"Did she hit you anywhere else?" I stepped in front of her, wanting to see her face, but Josie shook her head. "Has she done this before?"

Her face tightened as she hesitated, but I didn't need her to speak the words aloud to know this wasn't the first time Gwen had ever touched her daughter with violence.

Straightening, I pulled my hair out of its sweaty ponytail and redid it to make sure no strands were loose. Taking out my earrings, I placed them in Howler's palm. He didn't say anything, didn't ask what the hell I was doing. He knew.

He knew, and he wasn't going to stop me.

He wrapped his fist around my diamond studs before putting them in his front jeans pocket. Then he helped Josie fix her leotard. “Josie, you don’t have to be scared anymore. Your mom isn’t ever going to come near you again.”

“R-really?” Her little voice shook, and I saw the doubt in her eyes.

“Do you want to see her?” She shook her head, and Howler gave her the most reassuring smile he could muster. “Then you won’t have to. Daddy can promise you that much, baby girl.”

She threw herself into her father’s arms, hugging his neck and sobbing. “Th-thank y-y-you, D-d-daddy.”

My heart throbbing, I turned away from the sight that had the power to make me drop to my knees and walked over to the door. The clock on the wall told me it was time for parents to pick up their kids. Opening the door, I listened, waiting while my rage only festered and burned brighter with every passing minute.

By the time I heard Gwen’s voice, all the other girls were gone.

I stepped out of the classroom, making sure to shut the door behind me. Through the glass, Howler caught my gaze again and gave me a single nod. Turning, I started toward Gwen, barely noticing Barrick and Mia off to the side.

Seeing me, Gwen took a step back, fear in her eyes. But the bitch must have been on something or drunk off her ass, because she had the balls to smirk at me and run her mouth. "If it isn't the little puppy who's always chasing after my man. What's wrong, Lyla? Mad again because Howler won't touch you? Or is it that he knocked me up when he was supposed to be in love with you?"

I balled my hands into fists, her words only adding fuel to the inferno aflame inside of me. I wasn't even sixteen when Howler broke up with Gwen. It was weeks later that she told him she was pregnant. Maybe Howler had loved me then, but I was too young for him to even tell me his feelings. I wasn't going to hold that against him.

When I reached her, I finally let all the rage and chaos blowing like a hurricane inside of me loose on her. I didn't remember what I screamed at her or what I did to her. My anger was so strong, I blacked out.

She'd put her hands on Josie in violence. Why? Because Josie accidentally spilled juice on a new, expensive outfit? What a piece of shit.

By the time my rage had mostly burned out, Gwen was curled in the fetal position, sobbing that she was sorry and that it would never happen again. There was blood all over her and more bruises on her face and arms than Josie had marring her precious little body.

"You're right," I told her as I stood. "It won't ever happen again, because you won't ever see Josie again."

"Y-you can't take her away from me!" Gwen yelled, trying to get up. But the beating I'd just dished out had done a hell of a lot of damage. I wasn't sure, but I might have broken a few of her ribs and her wrist. "I-I'm her mother. She's mine."

"No. She's mine. You just gave birth to her." I bent at the waist and grinned at her, making her gulp in fright. "And if you ever come near her again, I'll fucking kill you."

two

Howler

Judge was already waiting at my house when we got there. When Lyla had called him requesting a cleanup crew, he'd told her he was on his way to my place with a doctor to examine Josie.

I didn't know if I wanted to put her through an ER visit, but I knew she needed to be checked over. Thankfully, my best friend had a solution for it with one of the doctors who stitched up and checked us over after fights in the Underground.

Turning off my SUV, I stepped out and opened the back door where Lyla was sitting beside Josie's booster seat. Josie was sound asleep, but Lyla hadn't wanted to be all the way in the front seat away from her in case Josie woke up and was scared. Both back doors had the child safety locks engaged in case Josie ever got adventurous. So far, she hadn't, but better safe than sorry.

Lyla was already unbuckling Josie's seat belt and then lifted her into her arms. Lyla still had that magic ability to not wake my daughter when she shifted her from one place to another, but now Lyla was stuck because she couldn't climb out of my huge SUV without falling.

I scooped her into my arms, solving her dilemma but causing one of my own.

I fucking loved having her there. Standing with both Lyla and Josie in my arms felt so damn right, all I wanted to do was savor it. Touching my forehead to the side of Lyla's, I breathed in deeply, getting a mix of her perfume and my little girl's baby shampoo.

The entire evening had been a nightmare. I didn't know if I could have handled it as calmly as I had without Lyla there to help me. She'd been so good with Josie, which didn't surprise me. But she'd kept her cool in front of my little girl before she couldn't take it any longer.

Then she'd kicked Gwen's ass. I didn't even get to see the final results, but I knew she must have done some major damage. I'd heard Gwen sobbing even through the closed classroom door. Thankfully, by then, Josie was already asleep, so she didn't hear her mother begging Lyla to stop.

One of Lyla's chilled hands touched the side of my face. "I'm sorry, but it looks like you're stuck with me for a while. I'm moving in with you until Josie is better."

"Jesus Christ, Lyla. I want you here. You know that." I touched my lips to her temple, torturing myself further. Her skin felt like silk against my lips, and I wanted to kiss every inch of her body to see if the rest of her was just as soft.

"I know what you want, Howler," she said so quietly I could barely hear her, even as close as we were. "The problem is, you don't have the nerve to take it."

Turning her head away, she glanced at my house. It was only about half as big as the one she'd grown up in with her brother, but it was still too big for just Josie and me. I'd built it myself after my dad died, leaving me responsible for his entire construction company. I was an architect, and Dad and I had always planned on being a team, but I was thrown a curve ball when he died.

When I designed this house, it was with the future in mind. Filling it with more kids, maybe a dog…

And Lyla.

Having Lyla share this house with me was something I'd always dreamed about but never allowed myself to hope for. Now that she was going to be staying with me for Josie's sake, I was going to be in the sweetest kind of hell.

Fighting back a groan, I carried them into the house. Judge met us at the door. The doctor was already in the living room, and I placed Lyla on the couch while she carefully woke up Josie.

The next hour was just as much of a nightmare as the previous few had been. Josie cried a lot and Lyla tried not to, but she couldn't hold back a few tears. Judge stood off to the side of the room so he wouldn't scare his goddaughter. His rage was just as powerful as my own, but Judge didn't have anyone to help him keep his in check.

When the doctor left, Lyla took Josie upstairs for a bath and to get her ready for bed. Josie had preschool Monday, Wednesday, and Friday every week. I told her she didn't have to go if she didn't want to, but she'd gotten upset. My girl liked school and playing with her friends, so I wasn't going to deny her if she actually wanted to go.

Fuck, who was I kidding? I wouldn't deny Josie anything. Ever.

As soon as Lyla and Josie were up the stairs, Judge walked over to stand beside me. "I'll have a court order by the morning to ensure Gwen no longer has even an ounce of custodial rights to Josie."

"I want her in jail," I gritted out.

"I would love to lock her up right now, Howler. But Lyla just fractured two of her ribs and broke the bitch's wrist. I can't have Gwen arrested, or it would put Lyla at risk. Give me a few weeks, let what happened tonight settle down, and then I'll find something on her. Fuck, even if I have to have someone plant drugs on her, I'll have her behind bars within a month. I promise."

Blowing out a frustrated breath, I nodded. "Yeah, okay. I don't want Lyla at risk any more than you do. Just do what you have to and make Gwen go away for as long as possible."

"I will, brother. I swear." He thrust his hands into the front pockets of his pants, his eyes going to the stairs where the girls had disappeared only minutes before. "I'm glad she's home. I've missed her."

"Me too," I admitted and waited for his reaction.

"You should have told her how you felt three years ago. She never would have left if you had."

Grimacing, he shook his head. "But it is what it is. You had your chance, and you blew it."

For a second, I was too stunned to respond. Then I grabbed him by his light-blue dress shirt and jerked him into my space. "What the fuck are you saying to me right now, Judge?"

My friend didn't even blink as he met my gaze. "I told you to do whatever you had to to make her stay. I meant anything. I wouldn't have gotten in your way if you'd told her you loved her back then. All I wanted was for her to stay. She's all I have, goddamn it. If being with you meant she stayed close so I could watch over her, then so be it."

"Why the hell didn't you say that at the time, huh?" I released him, shoving him back a few steps, pissed at my friend like never before. "When you said 'whatever,' I didn't think you meant…" I thrust my hands into my hair, hating him in that moment. "How did you even know how I felt about her? I made sure to never let you see."

He snorted. "I'm not blind. The agony on your face every time she's close to you is hard not to notice. But you fucked it all up, man. Because if you didn't have the guts to take what you wanted back then and convince her to stay, you don't deserve another chance now."

"Fuck you, Judge. I thought I would lose you and the Underground if I chose her."

He clenched his jaw, and he was the one to get in my face this time. "When you love someone, you risk it all. No matter the consequences. Loving a woman means she comes first. Over everything and everyone else. You failed, Howler. You proved to me that what you feel for my baby sister isn't strong enough."

"Get out before I do something I can't take back," I snarled at him, putting the length of the room between us. "Because I'm about to fucking kill you, Judge."

"Sucks, doesn't it?" he asked over his shoulder as he walked toward the door. "Knowing you were so close, and now you'll never get the girl."

"Who the hell said I wasn't going to get her?" I muttered as the door closed behind him.

I waited until I heard his car start and him driving away before I climbed the stairs. From the bathroom across from Josie's bedroom came the sounds of my daughter giggling. I paused in the open doorway, watching as Lyla lifted a handful of bubbles and placed them on Josie's head.

"Very pretty," Lyla said with a laugh. "Now, how about a bubble beard?"

"Like Barrick's?"

"Of course. If one must have a beard, then it must be perfection, just like Barrick's."

I watched the two of them for a moment, everything inside me aching. I could have had this every night for the last three years if I hadn't been so worried about losing everything else. Josie would have been happier, and fuck knows, I would have been too.

Judge was right. I didn't deserve a second chance because I hadn't been brave enough back then to fight for Lyla.

But that changed, starting now.

I would fight for her and lose everything—except for Josie—if I had to. Fuck the consequences.

Lyla was mine.

It was time everyone knew that.

three

Lyla

A heavy, warm hand touching my back had me snapping my eyes open as I jolted awake. Instinctively, my arms tightened around Josie, who was sound asleep curled up against me.

After her bath, I'd lain down on her bed to read her a book, but halfway through it, she'd started dozing off. By the time I was finished, she was snoring lightly, one of her little arms tossed over my middle. I'd been so comfortable and so damn reluctant to leave her, even to go down the hall to one of the guest bedrooms, that I'd let sleep take me right there in Josie's little twin princess bed.

Howler's scent hit me before his voice reached my ears. "Just making you more comfortable, baby," he murmured before scooping me up into his arms and carrying me out of his daughter's room.

“I was comfortable,” I told him when the door was closed behind him and I didn’t have to worry about waking Josie.

“For the moment, you were. Ten more minutes and Josie would have started tossing and turning like she does every night. Then you would have been thanking me.” He walked down the hall, in the opposite direction of the guest rooms.

“Wait, where are you going?” I demanded just as he opened the last door on the left. Walking in, he flipped the light switch with his elbow then kicked the door shut.

Blinking rapidly to get my eyes to adjust, I glanced around. The king-sized bed in the middle of the room caught my attention first. The dark tones of the pillowcases and duvet went well with the color of the walls. Nightstands stood on either side of the bed, with a lamp on each.

I guessed Howler slept on the left side of the bed because that was where the alarm clock was, along with a picture of him and Josie, both of them grinning at the camera, looking so much alike it made my heart clench.

"This is your room," I stated just as he placed me on the edge of the bed and pulled the covers back.

"Yup." Kicking off his shoes, he pulled his shirt over his head on his way to the connecting bathroom.

"Howler," I called after him, trying and failing to keep my eyes off his toned back.

"Yeah, babe?" he said over his shoulder, not turning around. He disappeared into the bathroom, and a moment later, I heard the shower turn on.

"Did you take something?" Getting to my feet, I followed him to the bathroom door and stopped, my mouth drying out at the same time my panties became drenched. I should have looked away, but I just couldn't bring myself to.

Not when he was standing completely naked beside the shower. His back was still to me, but fuck, his ass was the thing all my wet dreams were made of. My body suddenly felt like it was lit on fire as an ache began to throb between my legs. Pressing my thighs together, I tried to relieve some of the pain just looking at him was causing, but it did nothing to solve my problem.

He started to turn, and I knew I wouldn't survive so much as a peek at the front view. Turning away, I practically sprinted for the bedroom door.

I couldn't do this. It wasn't fair that he'd even teased me with something he would never willingly give. The bastard was tempting me with a dream I couldn't have. I didn't know whether to scream or cry.

Just as my fingers touched the knob, I was pressed up against the door. Howler's breath caressed my neck as he snaked his arms around my waist, locking me against his body as he pressed his front into my back, pinning me in place.

"Where do you think you're going?" he husked at my ear.

"O-one of the guest rooms." I gulped, trying to fight the breathlessness feeling his nakedness pressing into me was causing. "You're an asshole for bringing me in here when you know good and fucking well you won't—"

"Won't what?" he growled, kissing my neck before sinking his teeth into my flesh. "Won't touch you? Won't give you what your body is screaming for right now? Won't fuck you until neither of us can think straight?"

"All of the above," I gasped, arching my neck, silently begging for him to bite me again.

"That's where you're wrong, baby. Because as soon as I get this sweat off me, I'm going to crawl into that bed beside you and eat this pussy." He cupped my sex through my yoga pants and panties, groaning when he felt how wet I was. "I'm going to devour every drop of cream you've got to give me until you're writhing under my tongue. And then I'm going to put my cock right here." He pressed two fingers up into me through my clothes, circling them around my opening, making me moan and shudder against him. "You want that, don't you, Lyla baby?"

Helplessly, I nodded.

"Give me five minutes," he pleaded, kissing my shoulder. "And then I'll put us both out of our misery."

"I…" I licked my dry lips and moaned when I felt his cock flex against my hip. "I need a shower too. I was working out with Braxton earlier."

"You want to shower with me?"

"Honestly, I just want you to put your cock in me right now," I panted. "Up against this door, on the bed. I don't care where, as long as you are inside me. Now."

"I need to take my time with you," he muttered, kissing his way up my neck. "Don't want to hurt you, baby."

"You won't," I assured him, unable to keep the desperation out of my voice. Pressing back into him, I rocked my hips against his hard-on.

"But…" His fingers bit into my pelvic bone. "Your first time should be memorable."

"Our first time together will be, I swear. Please, Howler."

"No, I mean your first time, Lyla." His nose nuzzled my ear. "I'm harder than I can ever remember being. I don't want to hurt you when—"

My entire body went stiff, and I turned my head as far as possible so I could look at him over my shoulder. "Howler, do you think I'm a virgin?"

"Of course, you're a virgin. No way you would let anyone but me touch you."

Covering his hands, I pulled them off me and then turned so I could push him back. Surprised, he took two steps, his eyes narrowing on me as I glared up at him. "Here's the thing, Graham," I bit out, causing him to flinch at the use of his real name. "I got tired of you breaking my heart over and over again. Last Christmas, when you turned me down yet again, I went back to work after the winter break, and I gave my virginity to the first guy who was interested."

His face lost all color as his eyes shone with hurt so intense, it made me feel physically ill. "Are you fucking kidding me right now, Lyla? Because this joke is not funny."

"What isn't funny is having you blow hot and cold every two seconds. One minute, you look at me like I'm your entire world. The next, you can't run fast enough to get away from me." Tears burned my eyes, but I didn't try to hold them back. "And I am sick of it. I don't know what changed tonight, but I really don't trust you to wake up tomorrow and not freak out because, in your mind, we can't be together."

"That won't happen," he swore, taking a step toward me with his hand outstretched.

But I reached behind me and opened the door. "I know it won't. Because I won't let it."

"Lyla, just wait a second," he implored. "Let me tell you—"

"I'm not interested in whatever you have to say, Howler."

I backed through the door, keeping my gaze on his face because if I looked any lower, I knew I wouldn't be able to keep my focus. Or the resolve not to let what was about to happen continue. His being upset that I wasn't a virgin had saved me plenty of regrets come morning. I should have been thankful. Instead, my heart was aching too badly to be grateful.

four

Lyla

Josie went to school the next morning, despite both her dad and me trying to talk her out of it. I wanted her to see a therapist as soon as possible, get her started on the road to mental recovery after being abused by her mother. But she cried because she wanted to see her teacher and friends, so I didn't push.

Howler and I walked her in, and he pulled her teacher to the side to discuss the current situation and to make sure the woman knew not to let Gwen try to pick up Josie. Once he was satisfied no one would release his daughter to her mother or anyone else except him or me, he drove me to campus.

Neither of us spoke on the drive, but I could feel his gaze on me every few seconds. I kept my eyes focused out the passenger side window. For once, I had nothing to say. Not about what happened the night before, not the past, and definitely not about the future.

The hurt on his face when I'd told him I'd given my virginity to someone else had hit me the wrong way. I hated that I hurt him, but I hated him for pushing me away over the years.

My first time hadn't even been all that great. For one, part of me felt guilty, like I'd cheated on Howler, even though that was ridiculous. He'd been having sex with anyone who would willingly spread their legs for him for years. By the laws of whatever the fuck this was between us, if I'd cheated on him by giving up my virginity to some random guy, then he'd cheated on me hundreds of times.

He had no damn right to be mad or hurt over what I'd done.

"What time is your class over?" he finally asked less than a block from campus, his voice sounding hoarse from disuse.

"My last class ends at three." I pulled out my phone, texting Mia to see if she wanted to grab some coffee. No doubt one or both of my cousins would be joining us, but I didn't care to vent in front of them. Barrick already knew about my misadventure in hooking up after Christmas break, and Braxton wouldn't judge me. But I needed to talk to Mia, get perspective on all of this from another female.

"I'll pick you up then, and we can get Josie together."

"Is that a suggestion or a command?" I asked, keeping my tone neutral while not moving my gaze from my phone's screen.

"Fuck, Lyla. Don't be like this. I messed up last night. Trust me, I know that. But we need to talk. Seriously talk, not just brush over what happened." The SUV came to a stop, and he put it in park before unbuckling his seat belt and leaning toward me. Cupping the side of my face, he turned my head so I was looking straight at him instead of out of the corner of my eye. "I'm sorry, baby."

He stroked his thumb over my cheek, and it felt so damn good, my lashes started to lower in pleasure. But before I could give in fully, I unbuckled my seat belt and opened the door, getting away from him as quickly as I could before my heart took over and vetoed all of the smart things my brain was telling it.

"See you at three," I gritted out before slamming the door shut.

I still had to go to my dorm to get my books and then get to my first class of the day. While I was there, I grabbed my laptop and iPad as well, so I wouldn't have to make a return trip for them. I didn't know how long I was going to stay at Howler's, but I didn't want to rush it. If Josie needed me, then I would stay.

Even though being so close to her dad was torture, I would do it, just for her.

After my first class, I walked across campus to the café. Mia and Braxton were already there, coffees in hand while Brax devoured some kind of coffee cake that looked so good, my stomach growled.

Mia pushed a second slice and a cup of coffee my way with a wink, already knowing me so well that she'd guessed I would want a piece for myself.

Braxton dropped his fork onto his plate and wiped his mouth on a napkin before pinning me in place with his all-seeing dark eyes. "Mia said you need to vent. So, vent. We're all ears."

Mia elbowed him in the side. "Cool your jets, Captain Sensitive. Let the girl breathe first."

I took a sip of my coffee, sighing in pleasure that it was made perfectly. The taste lightened my mood somewhat, and I picked up my fork, digging into my afternoon snack. “Howler and I almost hooked up last night,” I announced around the bite of delicious cake.

Mia didn’t even blink, but Braxton strangled on the mouthful of coffee he’d just taken. Without looking at him, Mia pounded him on the back. “She said almost, Brax. Gods, relax a little.”

“I wouldn’t have cared if they had hooked up,” he rasped, wiping his mouth. “It’s that Howler had the balls to touch her that surprises the hell out of me. Dude is a killer in the cage, but when it comes to Lyla, he’s a total chickenshit.”

I pointed my fork at my younger cousin. “Truth,” I agreed before taking another bite.

“Whatever,” Mia grumbled. “So, tell us what happened and why it was an ‘almost hookup’ rather than an actual hookup.”

Washing down the bite of cake with another sip of coffee, I told them about what had gone down and why things had gotten so messed up. Mia wasn’t surprised when I admitted to hooking up with some guy right after Christmas, but Braxton was speechless for a moment.

"I'm kind of shocked, Lyla," he muttered with a shake of his head. "Seriously, I didn't think you would ever let any guy that close but Howler. I'm not judging. It's just that you've been in love with him since you were like fifteen or sixteen, and you never even looked at another guy in all that time."

No longer hungry, I pushed my half-eaten cake his way. Immediately, he grabbed the fork and started shoveling it into his mouth. "When I was home for Christmas break, Howler and I had a moment one night while I was visiting with Jo-Jo. But true to Howler form, he backed off before he could even kiss me. It pissed me off, and yeah, I'll admit it stung like a motherfucker. So, as soon as I got back to school, I decided enough was enough and went to a party, intent on hooking up and losing my V-card."

"Hey, it's yours to give to whomever you want," Mia said. "Howler lost his chance."

"Yeah," I muttered, frowning down at my cup of coffee. "So, why do I feel like I cheated on him?"

"Because you love the dumb bastard," Braxton told me with a grim shake of his head.

“I’m not denying that. I’m just so confused right now.”

“What are you confused about?” Barrick asked as he dropped down into the chair beside Mia. Without missing a beat, he kissed her on the forehead and picked up her coffee. Taking a swallow, he leaned back, studying me. “You need me to kick someone’s ass?”

I snorted. “I can kick anyone’s ass who needs it, thanks.”

“Then what’s the problem?”

I scooted my chair back and stood. “Mia and Brax can fill you in. I’ve got a class to get to.”

“Let me guess,” I heard him say as I walked out. “Howler is being a dumbass as usual.”

I didn’t stick around to hear how the other two replied. I walked to my class, getting there ten minutes early for once. But once class started, and the professor droned on and on about a subject I had no interest in learning, I tuned out everything and played with my phone in my lap.

By the time the professor dismissed us, I was bored out of my mind, had a new high score on Angry Birds Dream Blast, and was dreading facing Howler again. Grabbing my stuff, I walked toward where he'd dropped me off earlier, taking my time to delay the inevitable.

His SUV was already waiting. Seeing me coming, he jumped out of the driver's seat and walked around to open the passenger door for me. As he did, a group of girls walked by. They greeted him by name, and he nodded in acknowledgment but didn't even look twice at them. Instead, he looked right at me, and I nearly stumbled when I saw the unveiled hunger shimmering in his eyes.

"How was your day?" he asked as I neared.

"Boring," I grumbled, climbing up into the front seat.

"You could always quit and come work for me," he suggested. "I need someone to run the office who isn't afraid to tell me how it is."

"Your mom runs the office, and she isn't afraid to tell you to fuck off." I dropped my things on the floor at my feet and reached for my seat belt while he stood there watching me.

"She's been complaining about wanting to retire lately. If I had someone she trusted to take her place, she'd probably take a world cruise and never look back."

"I have a job," I reminded him, keeping my gaze straight ahead.

"True," he agreed. "But if you worked for me, Josie would see you every day."

I clenched my jaw. "You play dirty."

"With you, I have to." He leaned inside, his huge upper body taking up all my personal space. "Tell me you don't love me, Lyla. Tell me, and I'll back away. I won't mention what happened last night. I won't offer you a job. I'll go back to being the father of the little girl you adore and your brother's best friend. Say it, and nothing changes."

Closing my eyes, I sucked in a shuddering breath. My lungs filled with the scent of his body wash mixed with sweat and pure, delicious man. "I can't," I whispered.

"Thank fuck," he breathed half a second before his mouth crashed into mine.

five

Howler

Lyla's taste exploded on my tongue, and every primal instinct inside me roared to life. I cupped the back of her head and thrust my tongue deep, gorging myself on her essence.

She moaned into my mouth, her hands grasping my shirt and balling into fists, holding me in place.

For more years than I wanted to count, I'd stopped myself from kissing her time and time again. What a fucking idiot I'd been. Kissing Lyla was the most amazing, life-altering experience of my existence. It felt right. More so than anything else ever had or ever would.

Because she was mine.

With a willpower I didn't know I possessed, I pulled back enough to look at her. Slowly, dazedly, she lifted her lashes and licked her kiss-swollen lips. "I've wanted to do that since you were fifteen," I confessed. "And baby, the wait was fucking worth it."

"We have to pick up Josie," she reminded me, her voice shaking ever so slightly as she touched her fingertips to her bottom lip.

"Right," I agreed before kissing her again. This time, it was quick and hard, but no less soul-awakening. "Just to hold me over until we get home," I said with a wink. Stepping back, I shut her door and walked around to the driver's side slowly, taking my time so my jeans didn't crush my throbbing cock.

When I got behind the wheel, she was still touching her mouth, and I ached for just one more taste. But I knew if I kissed her again, we would end up being late to pick up Josie. Instead, I made do with gently grasping her wrist and pulling her hand away from her mouth. I kissed her fingers and laid her hand on my thigh before starting the vehicle and pulling into traffic.

At a red light, she lifted her hand from my leg to turn on the music. But when she started to sit back without replacing her hand where I'd positioned it, I caught it and put it back where it belonged.

"Are you going to tell me what changed last night?" she asked a moment later.

I didn't want to tell her about what Judge said the night before. "Last night, I opened my eyes," I told her instead, still being completely honest. "I'm tired of fighting what I feel for you. I want us to be together, and fuck the consequences."

She just sat there, studying me, probably trying to see if I was playing a game with her. After Judge's confession the night before, I realized he was right. I didn't deserve Lyla if I wasn't willing to put her first. I should have done this years ago, and I could have kicked my own ass for wasting so much time when we could have been together.

Lyla was still contemplating me quietly when I pulled into the parking lot of the private preschool Josie attended three days a week. Getting out, I walked around to the passenger side and opened the door. After looking at my outstretched hand for a moment, she took it, and I entwined our fingers as we walked inside to get our baby girl.

As soon as we walked into Josie's classroom, she came running over and threw herself into Lyla's arms. Lyla picked her up, kissing every inch of her face. My heart felt like it was going to explode in my chest at the rightness of the moment.

The teacher, Mrs. Miller, walked over to us with a smile on her face. “We had a very good day today, Mr. Bronson,” she assured me. Then her smile dimmed, and she lowered her voice. “Miss Hopkins tried to enter the building twice today. We changed her security code after our discussion this morning, so she wasn’t able to get in. The first time, there were no issues, but the second, we had to have security escort her off the premises.”

I looked over to where Josie was talking animatedly to Lyla about her day. “But Josie wasn’t upset?”

“She didn’t even know what was going on. I didn’t either until my boss informed me after the fact so I could talk to you about it.” She patted my arm comfortingly. “We just wanted to reassure you Josie is safe here and that her mother can’t get in to see her. You don’t have to worry about your child while she’s in our care.”

I gave her a grim smile, nodding. Still, in the back of my mind, I knew how conniving Gwen was. I’d been stupid enough to date her after all. She’d only been a distraction from what I really wanted when Lyla was far too young. Even back then, I knew I loved Lyla, and it drove Gwen crazy with jealousy because she suspected.

The shit she'd put Lyla through in the past because of that jealousy was the reason I'd broken up with her in the first place. Lyla held her own and gave it right back—times ten—but I wasn't going to let anyone mistreat her.

After gathering Josie's stuff, we left with Josie still in Lyla's arms. "Can we have spaghetti for dinner tonight?" she asked as Lyla buckled her into her booster seat.

"Sounds good. If Daddy says it's okay, we will."

"With Lyla's homemade garlic knots and salad." My stomach growled just thinking about it. "Let's stop at the grocery store and grab what we need," I suggested as I opened the passenger door and waited for Lyla to finish up.

"Yay!" Josie cheered and smacked a kiss on Lyla's cheek. "I really, really, really like you living with us, Lyla. It's like we're a family."

Lyla gave her a sweet smile before stepping back, but as she started to get into the front seat, I saw her chin tremble. As she settled into her seat,

I leaned in and kissed the corner of her mouth. "I like it too," I murmured close to her ear.

"Me too," she whispered, swallowing hard.

"What about dessert?" Josie asked from the middle of the back seat. "Can we have something yummy for dessert?"

"How about cookies?" Lyla suggested, turning in her seat so she could see Josie. She was all smiles again.

While Josie squealed in delight, I closed the door and walked around to the driver's side. They were still contemplating what cookies to make for dessert when I pulled into the grocery store a few minutes later.

"Chocolate chip."

"Boring," Josie said with a sass that matched Lyla's as we walked into the store. "What about birthday cake?"

"I've never made birthday cake cookies," Lyla informed her.

"I know how!" Josie assured her. "It's only sugar cookies with sprinkles. Uncle Judge's housekeeper's daughter showed me how."

Lyla's eyes widened, and she glanced at me. "When was Ellianna home?"

"She spent the summer here," I told her and watched as her face dropped in disappointment. Mabel's daughter was the same age as Lyla, and they'd basically grown up together. But when Ellianna went off to college, she didn't look back and was rarely home.

"How was she? Has she changed any?"

"I only saw her a few times, but yeah, she's changed some."

Lyla sighed, and I knew she was missing her childhood friend. But then she put a smile back on her beautiful face for Josie. "Well, I guess birthday cake cookies it is, then. Will you show me how to make them?"

"Don't worry, Lyla. I'll teach you." Josie danced around her happily. "Then we can make them every day!"

six

Lyla

After dinner, we all ate our cookies in the living room while watching a movie. Josie was obsessed with the *How to Train Your Dragon* movies, so we had the third one on already by the time Howler joined us with a glass of milk for each of us.

"Scoot," Howler told his daughter, who was sitting in the middle of the couch with her gigantic stuffed Toothless and Light Fury beside her.

Without a word, she scooted over. He looked at me next. "Scoot."

"You have the whole end of the couch to sit on. Why do I need to move?" I asked, stuffing a cookie into my mouth. Josie was right; birthday cake cookies were pretty incredible.

"Yeah, but you're on this end, and that's where I want to be." When I just lifted my brows at him, he huffed and bent to lift me. Sitting in my spot, he placed me beside him, then slung his arm over my shoulder, keeping me in place. "Ah, that's better." Picking up our glasses of milk, he offered me one then took a cookie off the plate on the side table. "Damn, these are good."

"Shh, Daddy. I can't hear," Josie scolded.

I smirked at him as he pressed his lips together. Reaching over him, I took two cookies off the plate and gave one to Josie. She smiled her thanks, and we each took a bite before she returned her avid gaze to the television. I knew for a fact that she'd seen this movie over a hundred times, yet she became engrossed in it like it was the first time every single time it was on.

"Come back here," Howler groused, tucking me into his side. He kissed the top of my head then got comfortable as he settled in to watch his daughter's favorite movie for the umpteenth time.

Tucking my socked feet up under me, I began to relax. Unable to help myself, I stuffed the rest of my cookie in my mouth and finished off my milk before placing the glass on the coffee table in front of us. When I leaned back, I rested my head on his shoulder and wrapped my arm around his waist, snuggling into his warmth as much as possible.

"Fuck," he groaned quietly, close to my ear. "This feels like perfection."

Smiling, I closed my eyes, enjoying the sensation even as I wondered how long our moment would last.

Halfway through the movie, Josie rested her head on my lap, and I combed my fingers through her hair the way I knew she loved. By the time the movie was over, she was sound asleep.

Carefully, Howler got to his feet and lifted her into his arms. "Be right back." But then he paused. "Unless you want to head up to bed now."

I stood, picking up our empty milk glasses and the plate that once held a dozen cookies. Josie and I had only had two each, but Howler had finished off the rest. "I have some homework to do before I go to bed," I told him as I started for the kitchen.

"Give me ten minutes, and I'll help you with it."

"You don't have to. I'm sure you're tired after working all day. You don't have to entertain me, Howler."

"I'll be back in ten," he repeated before climbing the stairs.

Rolling my eyes at his back, I pushed the door open to the kitchen and rinsed the dishes before putting them in the dishwasher. Our dinner dishes were already in there, so I started the cycle and wiped down the counters before grabbing my books and laptop and going back into the living room.

I had a paper due the following week, which I was only halfway done with. Opening the file, I read through what I had already written, editing as I went, then continued writing. History was one of the subjects I actually liked, and I had taken a class every semester at every college I'd attended over the past few years. I didn't need Howler's help with my homework, but I liked that he wanted to.

I was lost in what I was doing, so I didn't even hear him come down the stairs. It wasn't until he was sitting beside me that I realized he'd returned. "What's this paper about?"

"The fall of Constantinople."

"I'm going to pretend I know what or who that is," he muttered.

Laughing, I finally looked up from my laptop screen. "It was the capital of the Eastern Roman Empire."

"Right, and I'm bored with this topic already." He picked up the laptop off my legs and placed it on the coffee table. “Come here and make out with me instead.”

He picked me up just as easily as he had my computer and put me on his lap. I straddled his waist, my hands going to his shoulders to steady myself. I’d changed once we got home, and my running shorts and panties were already damp with my arousal.

“I-I should really get this paper finished.”

He stroked his long fingers down my neck, making me shiver. Why did his every touch have to feel so damn good? “There’s plenty of time for that later. Right now, I need another taste.” Cupping the back of my head, he pulled me down until our mouths were only a breath away from touching. “So sweet,” he breathed. “I don’t think I’ll ever get enough.”

“Howler,” I moaned, pressing my wet pussy down on his lap, thrilling at the feel of his hardness pulsing against my core. “Please.”

With a low, feral growl, he captured my mouth with his. The moment his tongue brushed against mine, I felt light-headed. He tasted like the cookies he had gorged on and something more potently addictive than sugar. Hungrily, I kissed him back.

I stabbed my hands through his shaggy, dark-blond hair, desperately trying to make the kiss last forever.

His huge hands fell to my ass and cupped each hip, squeezing roughly before pressing me down into his hardness even more. A helpless whimper escaped me, only to be swallowed by his continued kiss, and I rubbed myself against him.

"Fuck, fuck, fuck," he bit out as he pulled back. "We have to take this upstairs because I'm about to go off in my damn jeans."

His confession made me stupidly happy. I loved that he didn't have control over his body with me. "So, take me upstairs," I commanded.

"Yes, ma'am." His hands still gripping my ass, he stood, and I wrapped my legs around his waist. As he climbed the stairs with ease, I attacked his neck, licking and nipping, memorizing how each part of his body tasted.

"Baby, please. I'm only so strong," he groaned, his fingers contracting on my ass. "You keep that up, and I'm gonna fuck you up against the wall."

"Sorry, I'll be good," I lied, sinking my teeth into his earlobe. He shuddered so forcefully, my own body shook.

A savage curse escaped him, and he took off running, making me giggle as the purest kind of happiness exploded in my chest. This was happening. Howler and I were about to be together, and I couldn't contain the excitement and joy that were mixing with the intense need that had been consuming me for years.

The wait had been pure agony, and I still wasn't sure what would happen come morning, but all I could think about right then was how good it was going to be when Howler physically became a part of me.

His door was pushed open, then kicked shut, and he sprinted to his bed. My back hit the mattress, and he came down on top of me, his mouth fusing to mine. Our hands busily tore at each other's clothes, and I heard my shorts rip. Another powerful tug and my panties went with them.

As soon as the bottom half of my body was exposed, he thrust two fingers into me. I moaned, finally breaking the kiss. I lifted my hips, arching up into his touch as my legs began to tremble. He wasn't gentle with me; each thrust was rough, desperate almost.

And I loved it.

Howler's thumb grazed over my throbbing clit, and my orgasm hit me.

"Shh, shh," he murmured, kissing my brow tenderly even as he continued to thrust his fingers into me roughly, drawing out my release. "I've got you, baby."

When I could breathe again, I grabbed his head and pulled him in for another kiss. "My turn," I said with a wicked grin as I slid out from under him.

"Whatever you want, Lyla." Rolling onto his back, he spread his arms wide, giving me permission to do anything and everything I'd ever dreamed of doing to and with him.

Straddling his waist, I pulled my T-shirt over my head then unfastened my bra. The straps fell down my arms. Meeting Howler's eyes, I let the bra slowly fall away. A hiss escaped him, and I smirked down at him. "Like what you see?"

"You have no fucking idea." His callused hands cupped each breast, his rough skin skimming over my hard nipples.

I moaned his name, my head falling back, but when he started to lift up, I quickly pushed him back down. "Still my turn," I chided.

"Right. I'll just lie here and die a happy man while you torture me to death." Winking, he folded his arms behind his head. "I'm yours."

My heart did a silly little flip, but I quickly pushed that aside and started making some of my fantasies about this man a reality. Pushing all my hair to one side, I bent, kissing his chest. I licked each pec, letting my teeth scrape over his flat nipples, earning me another curse from him.

Grinning against his skin, I moved my lips to the center of his chest and pressed a deep kiss right over his heart. It was pounding furiously, and as I moved lower, my hair tickling over his abdomen, I could hear the beat grow even louder.

I traced my tongue over his hard eight-pack, then down to the top of his unbuttoned jeans. While he'd been tearing the bottom half of my clothes off me, I'd only gotten as far as unzipping and unbuttoning him. Pushing back the sides of the material, I kissed the top of his low riding boxer briefs. Lifting my head, I watched him through my lashes as I pushed my hand underneath his clothes and wrapped my fingers around his massive shaft.

"Mother of God," he groaned, his eyes closing in agonized pleasure. "Baby, please. I'm so fucking close right now."

Releasing him, I quickly got rid of the rest of his clothes, then did the one thing I'd always wanted to do. Gripping him in a tight fist, I lowered my head and touched my tongue to the very tip, licking away the pearly white drops that were already leaking out.

He jerked, groaning my name, and clenched one of his hands in my hair. Taking him in my mouth, I went down halfway before he hit the back of my throat. His hand in my hair pulled me back, and with a curse, he twisted us so I was once again on my back and he was between my legs.

Fisting himself in one hand, he spread my pussy lips with the other and pushed into me balls deep in one thrust. We both groaned at his invasion. I felt stretched to the limit, unable to breathe without my inner walls contracting around him, welcoming him home.

"You're so damn tight," he panted. "This pussy is paradise, baby. I don't ever want to leave it."

I felt myself creaming around his cock, and he pulled back, only to thrust back in so hard, I saw stars. My nails bit into his sides, and he growled his pleasure before latching on to one of my nipples.

"Howler," I cried out.

"Lyla, I fucking swear, I'm going to come right now if you keep saying my name like that." He pressed his forehead to mine, breathing hard as he thrust into me faster. "I've wanted this for too long, and you feel so damn good."

"So do you," I told him with a whimper as he pulled his cock out and slammed it back into me. He was so thick and long, and I was so stretched, every move he made, every breath he took, sent off little ripples of pleasure inside me that were pushing me higher and higher toward another release.

I loved how rough and hard he was being, that he wasn't treating me like I was fragile. His heavy, muscular body was pounding me into the bed, while the room filled with our shared moans and heavy breathing.

“Baby, look at me.” Without hesitation, I lifted my lashes and met his passion-glazed eyes. “I love you.” The words came out in a reverent rasp.

The breath felt like it was knocked out of me, tears burning the backs of my eyes. I never thought I would ever hear him say those three little words. “I-I love you too.”

“Lyla.” Ravenously, he kissed me, and just as his tongue brushed against mine, I came.

My release was even more powerful than my first, and it almost hurt as my pussy contracted around his cock. Above me, Howler went still, his entire body tensing as his arms shook.

Sweat dripping down his brow, he reared back his head and roared my name.

seven

Howler

Half asleep, I reached for Lyla in the dark.

Only to come into contact with a chilled, empty bed.

I opened my eyes and glanced around, keeping my ears open to listen for any sign of her. The light was off in the bathroom, but the one in the hall was on. Sitting up, I hit the switch on the lamp beside the bed. "Baby?" I called out, but I got no answer.

Getting out of bed, I grabbed a pair of basketball shorts out of my dresser and walked down the hall to check on Josie. The door to her room was cracked open, letting the hall light stream in enough to show both my girls were sound asleep on Josie's twin princess bed. Josie's blond hair was spread over Lyla's arm, her face pressed into Lyla's chest. Lyla's other arm was wrapped around Josie's tiny body, holding her close and protectively to her.

Noticing the covers had been kicked off them, I walked quietly into the room and tucked the comforter up around them both. Lyla had on one of my shirts, her hair a tangled mess across the pillows. Instinct screamed at me to carry her back to our bed and fuck her over and over again, but she looked exhausted and content.

Bending, I kissed her forehead, then Josie's, and exited the room, closing the door behind me. Knowing I wouldn't get any more sleep that night, I walked downstairs and made sure the house was locked up. Normally, I couldn't fall asleep until I knew the house was secure and Josie was safe enough for me to get some rest. But after the double fuck session with Lyla, I'd passed out as soon as she'd fallen on top of me after riding my cock until we were both shaking with our shared release.

I fell asleep with her slight weight and scent enveloping me in contentment.

Opening the back door that led from the kitchen into the garage, I made sure my Harley was there and that the door was down. There was plenty of room beside my motorcycle for a car, but my SUV was too long for me to park it in there.

Closing the door, I locked it then walked through the rest of the house. I double-checked the front door then the French doors that opened up onto the deck. I had a huge backyard with a privacy fence. I'd designed and built Josie a playset that included a princess tower, two different slides, and a swing set.

With how cold it had been lately, though, Josie hadn't been out there much. Which was why I was surprised when I found the doors unlocked. I'd checked those same doors religiously every night, and they had been locked the night before. Josie hadn't even had time to go outside earlier since she was helping Lyla cook and then went straight from her bath to watching a movie.

Paranoid that my girls weren't safe, I locked the French doors, then walked through the entire house, checking every room. Nothing was out of place, but I still felt like something was off.

Heart pounding, I went back to Josie's room. She and Lyla were still sound asleep, but I felt uneasy. Quietly, I walked through the darkened room to her closet, needing to make sure every hiding place was checked before I could breathe easier.

Jerking the closet door open, I was prepared to fight, but it was empty. Yet…

I could smell her fucking perfume.

It was the same strong scent Gwen had worn from the time I'd met her, and one I couldn't get rid of even long after we broke up. In the end, I'd bought new pillows and bedding, yet it still had lingered in the apartment I'd lived in at the time. Smelling it now made my stomach clench with anger.

That crazy bitch had been in my house. In Josie's room, her goddamn closet.

And I hadn't even suspected.

I should have, though. She was psychotic, and now that I'd blocked her from seeing Josie, she would be looking for another way to get to her. Maybe even take her from me. Not because she wanted Josie, but because she hated me and knew Josie was my entire world.

"Howler?" Lyla's soft voice made me jerk in reaction.

Sucking in a deep breath to calm my rage, I walked over to the bed where she was still curled up with my daughter. "Sorry I woke you, baby," I told her quietly as I bent to kiss her lips.

“Josie had a bad dream,” she explained. “She was crying, and I didn’t want to wake you.”

“Hold on to her tight,” I ordered. Her arms tightened around Josie’s body, and I lifted them both into my arms.

After carrying them down the hall to my room, I shut the door with my foot before placing them in the center of the bed. Leaving them only for a second, I locked the door, then climbed in behind Lyla.

Once my arms were able to wrap around them both, I finally began to relax. “I was just checking the doors,” I whispered close to Lyla’s ear. “The French doors were unlocked.” I felt her stiffen and she turned her head, but I could only make out the outline of her face in the dark. “Gwen was in Josie’s room. I could smell her perfume in the closet. Like she was hiding in there for a while or something.”

“Do you think she was in there while we were—” She broke off, but I knew what she was thinking.

“I don’t know, baby.”

"What if Josie's bad dream wasn't a bad dream?" she whispered. "What if Gwen was in there and—"

"Shh, shh," I murmured, kissing her temple to calm her. "We can ask Josie in the morning. The house is locked, and I made sure it was empty. I'll have all the locks changed tomorrow and a few more added to the French doors. We should also talk to Judge about getting a restraining order."

I felt her nod.

"Don't worry, baby. I'm not going to let Gwen hurt anyone I love."

"I'm not scared of her. But I will kill her if she tries to touch Jo-Jo again," she swore.

"I know you will." Kissing her again, I tightened my arm over the two people who mattered the most to me. "Get some sleep. I've got you."

***

Both my girls were still sound asleep when I got up for work the next morning, but I couldn't leave the house with them sleeping inside and no one to watch over them.

While I was making coffee, I called Judge and told him what had happened the night before with the unlocked door. After the conversation we'd had a few nights prior, there was no way in hell I was going to tell him the other part. Not yet. I'd deal with him regarding Lyla and me when I had to.

He assured me he would send someone over to watch the house, and I waited until I saw one of Judge's people pull into my driveway before leaving.

My mother was already in the office when I got to work. The place smelled like perfectly brewed coffee and her delicate perfume as I walked in with a set of new plans in hand for the latest development we were working on.

Seeing I was alone, she narrowed her eyes on me. "Where's Josie?" she demanded, her hands on her hips.

Dressed in a pair of jeans and a chic floral top, Cherie Bronson didn't look like anyone's grandmother. Fuck, she barely looked old enough to be my mother. After my father's death, she'd started to age rapidly from the loss of the love of her life, but when Josie was born, it was like she was given a new beginning.

She had more energy, smiled all the time, and it had worked miracles. My mother had aged backward overnight, losing at least a decade of age in appearance when the gloom that surrounded her like a dark cloud had lifted and even took away some weight in the process.

"She's at home with Lyla. They were both still sleeping this morning, and I didn't want to wake them." I kissed her on the cheek before continuing on to my office.

She followed, closing the door as she entered behind me. I sat down behind my desk, whistling to myself as I went through the stack of messages already waiting on me.

"All right, mister. What's going on with you?"

At the sound of her mom tone, I lifted my gaze from the message in my hand to her. "What?"

"You are whistling and walking around with a new strut to your step, Graham. So, I will repeat—what is going on with you?"

"Nothing is going on with me," I evaded, picking up the phone to return a call that needed my immediate attention.

"Graham Bronson," she snapped, and my finger hovered over the last number on my desk phone. "Put the damn phone down and talk to your mother right now, boy. You might be grown, but you aren't so big I won't put you over my knee and whip your ass."

I fought a grin, knowing she wasn't kidding. She would try to whip me, and I'd end up letting her because I wouldn't risk her hurting herself. "Lyla is staying at my house," I told her.

"And? I already knew that." She'd been giddy about it the day before when I'd told her, until she found out why Lyla was staying at my place. Then I'd had to talk her out of finding Gwen and committing murder.

"And," I began but paused, not sure if I was ready to tell my mom I'd fucked the girl she had always wanted me to spend the rest of my life with. She loved Lyla like another daughter and had made it very plain where she stood on the two of us getting together.

"Graham!" she growled, and I laughed.

"Something may or may not have happened with us last night," I admitted. "But if you even hint to Judge about it—"

Mom was practically dancing with happiness now, and she quickly waved off my comment about Judge. "All the power that boy was given after his father died has gone to his head. He's got a total complex now and needs to realize he can't dictate everyone's life. Especially his sister's."

Coming around my desk, she kissed my cheek. "I'm so happy for you, sweetheart. Just don't fuck it up. Lyla is exactly what you and Josie need. And if you lose that girl, I'll disown you."

Leaving that threat hanging over my head, she walked out of my office. I shook my head at her retreating back, picked up the phone once again, and got to work.

But even as I was returning phone calls to clients who needed my full attention, I couldn't stop thinking about the night before. Being with Lyla was everything I'd ever fantasized it would be, but I couldn't help wondering if she was sore this morning.

I should have been gentler with her, taking things slower. But once I had her in my arms, I'd lost it. And instead of making love to her the way I'd always planned, I'd fucked her hard.

A sudden realization hit me in the middle of an important phone call, and I quickly made an excuse before hanging up and grabbing my cell.

"Hello?" Lyla said groggily.

"Are you on any kind of birth control?" I demanded, unable to hide the panic in my voice.

There was a pause on her end before her sassy voice filled my ear. "Good morning to you too, sunshine. I slept so well. How about you?"

Groaning, I leaned back in my desk chair. "Baby, I'm sweating right now. Please, just tell me you're on something. I forgot protection last night. Both damn times."

"Actually, I'm not," she informed me, making my stomach clench in dread. "But you can stop sweating. I'm clean. As for pregnancy, that isn't a problem either. It's not the right time for me."

"I'm clean too," I rushed to assure her, relieved she wasn't freaking out. "I got tested six months ago, and I haven't been with anyone in over a year."

"Glad that's cleared up." She yawned. "I'm going back to sleep."

"Wait." I stopped her, wanting to hear her voice for a little longer. "One of Judge's people is in the driveway."

"Why?" she demanded, sounding irritated. "You know I'm trained to protect myself and others, right? It's kind of my job."

"Because I couldn't leave for work knowing the two people I love the most were sleeping and vulnerable to my crazy-ass ex. And I don't care how much training you have, I'm not leaving you unprotected."

"Okay, then," she said after a moment, sounding dazed.

"Do you want me to come home at lunch and eat with you and Josie?" I asked, changing the subject.

"I could bring you something," she suggested hesitantly.

"Whatever you want, baby."

"What I really want is for you to be cuddled in bed with us again, but reality is a bitch and you're at work already." I grinned, picturing her pouting. "I'll bring you lunch. That way, Josie can stay with Cherie afterward. I have an afternoon class I have to go to."

"All right. Just bring me some of the leftover spaghetti from last night." My desk phone rang, and I blew out a frustrated sigh. "I have to go."

"Don't yell at anyone," she cautioned.

"I'll try my best, baby." Still holding the phone to my ear, I picked up the landline. "This is Graham. Please," I gritted out before the person on the other end could answer, "hold a moment."

Her laughter was my reward for attempting to be polite. "I'll see you in a few hours," she promised.

"Be careful. Love you."

Her quick inhale made my cock instantly hard. "I love you too," she murmured softly before hanging up.

Tossing my cell on the desk, I put the landline back to my ear. "Yeah, what is it?"

eight

Lyla

I hated driving.

I had a car at my brother's house that had only been driven a handful of times ever. I was a fairly good driver and had never personally been in an accident. But when I was in high school, I saw someone else wreck right in front of me, and I'd been anxious behind the wheel ever since.

Judge's security guy, Tony, drove Josie and me to Howler's office downtown. I had an entire lunch packed for the three of us so we could eat together before I went to class. With Josie's hand in one of mine and our food in the other, we walked in, only to have Cherie, Howler's mother, greet us.

"There's my sweet girl," she said, swooping down to kiss Josie's cheek. "How's my baby feeling today?"

"Grandma, Lyla made spaghetti last night, and we get to eat leftovers with Daddy," she told her excitedly.

"Yummy. It smells so good." Cherie straightened and hugged me. "Good to see you, love. Go on in. He's been growling at people for the last hour, so maybe seeing you two will put him in a better mood."

"Do I want to know why he's all growly?" I asked with a grimace.

Cherie glanced down at Josie then sighed quietly. "I'm sure he will tell you."

Figuring it had something to do with Gwen, I nodded and scooped Josie into my arms. "Tell Grandma you'll see her after lunch, Jo."

"See you, Grandma," she said with a wave as we walked into her father's office.

The door to Howler's office was closed, so I knocked twice before opening it. Walking in, I put Josie on her feet, and she skipped over to his desk. "Daddy, we brought you leftovers and salad."

He lifted her onto his lap and kissed the top of her head. "Thank goodness. My stomach sounds like there is a bear in there. Shh, listen. I bet you can hear him."

Giggling, she kissed his cheek.

He put her on her feet as he stood, then slowly crossed to me. As I watched him through my lashes, he ran his eyes over me hungrily from head to toe. Licking his lips, he stopped only a few inches away. "Fuck," he muttered low enough so Josie wouldn't hear him from where she was now sitting in his chair at the desk. "I've missed you all damn day."

Pleasure filled my chest, and I stepped into his personal space. "I missed you too," I confessed. "Is that why you've been growling at everyone? Or did something happen?"

Wrapping his arms around my waist, he buried his face in my neck. "Let's talk about that later," he said close to my ear. "When little ears can't overhear."

I pulled back enough to see his face. "Is it that bad?"

He shrugged, his face tense. I stroked a finger down his nose, wanting to erase the worry lines forming there. "Nothing's going to happen to Josie," I promised him. "No matter what."

Closing his eyes, he pressed his forehead to mine. "You're amazing, you know that? I love you so damn much."

Even though it wasn't the first time he'd said those words since last night, my heart exploded with joy like it was. "Are you hungry?" I asked, needing to distract us both before I kissed the breath out of him right there in front of Josie.

"Starving," he said with a groan, but I wasn't sure if he meant for food or me, because I could feel just how hard he was pressing into my belly.

Grinning, I stepped back and started pulling containers out of the bag I'd packed for us. "I made fresh garlic bread this morning since I couldn't go back to sleep after you called. Then Josie helped me make a salad to go with our spaghetti."

"It smells amazing." Moving around the desk, he started clearing a spot for the three of us to eat, while I set out our individual dishes.

Josie sat in her father's chair, and the two of us took the two guest chairs in front of the desk. She kept us entertained with conversation while we ate, distracting us both from whatever was bothering Howler, but I could feel the tension practically radiating off him as our meal came to an end.

Once we were done eating, I put everything away and then took Josie into the bathroom to help her wash the spaghetti sauce off her face. With her face freshly clean, I left her with Cherie before going back into Howler's office.

"I'll pick you up when your class is over," he said before I could speak. "Just text me when you're done."

"I can just get a ride to your place from Barrick or call for the town car," I told him.

"No. I'll pick you up." Pulling me against him, he kissed me. It was a quick kiss, but it still left me breathless when he lifted his head. "Mom's going to watch Josie tonight and tomorrow night, and Judge is going to put someone on her house to make sure nothing happens."

There was something in his tone that had the fine hairs on my body rising. Josie spending the night with Cherie wasn't unusual; I knew that. But there was just something…off. "Howler, what's going on?"

Exhaling heavily, he dropped down into his chair and reached for my hand, his fingers playing with mine before he brought them to his lips and finally answered. "After I called your brother this morning, he decided to have someone follow Gwen. The guy found her coming out of one of the drug dens on the south side of town. From there, she walked to a house a few blocks away, and when she left, the guy thought he saw a gun barrel sticking out of her tiny-ass purse."

"I'm not going to class," I told him, starting to shake. A gun. Gwen had a gun. Fuck. Was she that desperate to take Josie away from her father? If she came near my little Jo-Jo, I was going to kill her. "I'll take Josie home with me. I won't let that bitch anywhere near her."

"The gun was for you," he said, stopping me in my tracks. "Judge's guy went in and talked to the people in the house. After a little incentive, they all told him Gwen was ranting and raving, high off her ass, and saying she wanted to teach you a lesson. She wants to hurt you, Lyla."

An indelicate snort left me. "Like that cunt has the guts to come at me, even with a gun."

"Maybe she would, maybe she wouldn't. But I'm not taking any chances. Josie is going to my mother's tonight and—"

"Wait," I stopped him, holding up my hand. "If Gwen is after me, then Josie shouldn't have to leave her home. I'll just go back to the dorm or stay with Judge."

"The fuck you say!" he exploded. "You are going to be where I can see for myself that you're safe. Where *I* can protect you. Me. Not Judge."

"I can protect myself."

"I. Don't. Care!" he roared, backing me against the door of his office.

"I'm not fragile, Howler."

"How many times do I have to tell you, baby?" Lowering his head, he brushed his lips lightly over mine. It was a tease of a kiss, but damn if it didn't make me light-headed. "I protect you because you are one of the two most precious people in my world, not because you're fragile."

Everything inside me melted. I didn't want to be dependent on anyone, yet I loved that Howler wanted to take care of me. Wrapping my arms around his neck, I pushed up onto my tiptoes and kissed him, long and hard. He grabbed my ass and lifted me, and I wrapped my legs around his hips.

"I can't fuck you against this door when my mom and daughter are on the other side, baby," he muttered, irritable. "But tonight, I'm going to fuck you so hard, neither of us will be able to walk tomorrow."

My head fell back against the door, and I clung weakly to his shoulders. “Howler,” I mewled. “I want you so bad.”

“Me too, baby. Me too.” He kissed his way down my neck, only stopping when he got to my shirt. With a growl, he attacked my mouth when he ran out of bare skin. “But we can’t.”

“Then stop kissing me,” I challenged. “You’re making me so wet, I won’t be able to walk around campus.”

“Don’t go. Stay here.” He lifted his head, his eyes seeing too much of what I didn’t want to share with the world. “Do you even want to go to college?”

I knew the answer I was supposed to give. *Yes, I wanted to go to college. It was where you were supposed to find out new truths about yourself. Spread your wings and live it up while you could.*

Only, I’d spread my wings, I’d found out all the truths about myself I was ever going to find. But all those dreams I’d ever had, all the wants and desires and plans for the future, they never changed even when I was thousands of miles away from home.

I didn't want college. I wanted Howler and Josie. I wanted a house and a dog running around the backyard. I wanted a family I could call my own, kids clinging to my leg, and Josie calling me "Mom." I wanted a ring on my finger and a husband who would move heaven and earth just to be with me.

And I suspected Howler already knew all of those things about me.

Only he hadn't moved heaven and earth to be with me. He hadn't done much of anything other than fuck my brains out. I'd gotten the words from him, that sweet "I love you" pledge, but maybe I should have been disgusted with myself for letting him have me so easily.

Part of me kind of was.

Yet I was too lost in finally being with him, getting to taste him and hold him, and calling him mine for the moment that I didn't give a single fuck.

"Lyla?" His voice had lowered and became more imploring. "My offer to take over Mom's job is always open. I'll give you whatever salary you ask for and anything else you want."

I put on my best smile and shook my head. "As tempting as that offer is, I'm going to have to pass." I kissed him, keeping the contact quick and soft before unwrapping myself from around him. "I need to get to class."

Groaning, he nodded. "Yeah, okay. Be vigilant. Don't go looking for trouble. And stay in a crowd. I will pick you up as soon as you text me." Placing his hand at the small of my back, he walked me out of his office.

As I passed Cherie's desk, I stopped to give her a hug and kiss Josie. "Looks like you're spending the night with Grandma tonight, kiddo," I told her as she slung her little arms around my neck.

"Oh," she said with a pout. "But will you still be at my house when I get home?"

I kissed the tip of her nose. "I will. I promise. You be good, and when you get home, we can make those birthday cake cookies again."

Her entire face lit up, and she gave me a smacking kiss on the cheek. "I will. I promise. Bye, Lyla. Love you."

"Bye, sweet girl. See you soon."

As he walked me out to the car I'd come in earlier, Howler stroked his hand down my back. "It's my turn to make you dinner tonight."

My eyes widened. "You can cook? I thought you had a housekeeper who did that for you."

"Sometimes. But I can cook just as well as you can." Opening the back door of the sedan where my brother's guard was waiting, he touched his lips to my temple. "Be good and stay safe."

"You too," I said with a smirk. "Get some work done, lazy."

Laughing, he kissed my lips then stepped back. "I love you."

I couldn't get over him saying those three words to me so easily. Each time caused an explosion of pleasure to detonate in my chest. "I love you too."

nine

Lyla

I was walking out of class, my phone already out to text Howler I was ready to go, when I caught sight of my brother standing outside the door.

Putting my phone back in my bag, I walked over to him, curious why he would show up on campus out of the blue.

Seeing me coming, he opened his arms wide, and I walked into them, hugging him tightly. "What's up?" I asked when I stepped back, smiling up at him.

Growing up, it was just the two of us, even when our father was still alive. Our dad was a mean sonofabitch, using his fists on anyone who got in his way whenever he was drinking. Our mother stayed out of the line of fire, but I didn't learn my lesson until I was almost a teenager. Before that, though, Judge would put himself between the old bastard and me whenever I happened to find myself in the wrong place at the wrong time.

He wasn't just my brother. To me, he was the only true father figure I'd ever had. The one person in the world I knew loved me without exception. His overprotectiveness had never really bothered me because I knew he was only doing what his instincts told him to do—protect those he loved the most.

Which, sadly, was me and very few others.

Dropping his arm around my shoulders, he guided me toward the door. "You got time for a coffee? I didn't know your schedule, so I called Braxton to see where you were."

"Sure. I always have time for you," I assured him as we stepped out into the chilly fall afternoon.

As we walked toward the campus café, he kept glancing around, keeping an ever-watchful eye out for danger. I sighed. "Relax. Gwen doesn't have the guts to do anything to me."

"Gwen is a deranged cokehead who doesn't know up from down on a good day, but she's vindictive. She knows she can't touch you. You destroyed her the other night, and she knows no one will let her near you even if she tried. That's why she got the damn gun."

I rolled my eyes so hard, I almost gave myself a headache. "Oh please, like that cunt knows how to use one."

"Lyla!" he snapped my name. Stepping in front of me, he grasped my shoulders and shook me ever so slightly. "Listen to me. You don't know what Gwen is capable of. None of us do. She bought a goddamn gun and was telling people she wants to make you pay. Even though he had primary custody, Howler was still paying her child support for when she had Josie overnight. That's stopped now. Her booze and drug money are obsolete, and she wants to blame anyone but herself. She's chosen you to be the villain in this, honey. You are her target."

I shrugged off his hands. "I'm not scared of her."

His laugh was dry as he shook his head at me exasperatedly. "Of course you aren't, but you should be. She's not stable."

Not wanting to spend the time I had with him arguing, I changed the subject. "You didn't tell me Ellianna was home over the summer."

His entire face shut down, just as I knew it would, closing me off from everything he was thinking. I didn't know what his deal was. I loved Ellianna like a sister, but he couldn't even bring himself to speak of or even to her when she was around.

"I barely noticed she was there," he said with a new coldness to his tone that made me want to smack him upside the head. "I guess I forgot about her."

"Why are you such a jerk to her, Judge? Mabel treats us like we are her own children, and you can't even be nice to her actual child for a single moment?"

"She doesn't respect me," he countered, sounding like a petulant child.

"Because she doesn't call you Judge?" I laughed. "Who cares if she calls you Zachary or Mr. Bennet or whatever the fuck else? You're so full of yourself, you know that?"

His jaw tensed, but I just linked my arm through his and started walking again. "Come on. I want some coffee before I call Howler."

"There's no need to call Howler," he grumbled. "I'll take you home."

I lifted my brows. "His home or ours?"

"Ours, of course. Why would you go to his? Josie is at Cherie's for the next two days. You have no reason to be at his house when she's not there."

I stopped right in front of the main entrance to the café. Crossing my arms over my chest, I glared up at my brother. "Last time I checked, I was twenty years old and didn't need to ask anyone's permission if I wanted to have a sleepover with a member of the opposite sex."

Judge's face twisted with disgust. "I don't want to think about my baby sister having any sleepovers with any worthless douchebag, least of all my best friend."

"Whether you want to think about it or not, I'm still going to Howler's tonight. He and I…" I paused, unsure how to explain to my brother what had happened without damaging either of our psyches. I didn't want to just blurt out that I'd fucked his best friend the night before. Hell, I didn't want to put those mental images in his head any more than he wanted me to. "We're together, Judge," I finally modified.

"No," he snapped, his face twisted with pure anger. "I forbid it."

"Excuse you?" I poked him in the chest. "You don't get to forbid me to do anything. Ever. I'm your sister, not your servant. Or anything else, for that matter. Your sister, asshole."

"You're right. I can't forbid you. I apologize." But before I could even start to be mollified, he pulled out his phone. After doing something to the screen, he placed it to his ear, and my stomach dropped even before he spoke. "Howler, Lyla says you two are together." He paused to listen, and I grabbed his wrist, pulling the phone away from his ear enough so I could listen.

There was a pause before Howler released a drawn-out breath. "Yeah?"

Closing my eyes, I waited for my brother to drop the bomb and make Howler choose. I held my breath, because even though Howler had said he loved me multiple times, he wouldn't be picking me.

"Never mind," Judge said after a moment, and my eyes snapped open. But my brother wasn't even looking at me. His gaze was on something in the distance, and I could feel a new tension settling into his muscles. "We'll discuss this later. I have to go."

"What?" I asked, dazed from the sudden reprieve I'd been given. For the moment, at least.

Pocketing his phone, he turned away from the café and steered me toward the parking lot. "I'll drop you off at Howler's," he announced. "I have something I need to do."

"What's going on?" I demanded. "Who did you just see that has put you in this weird mood all of a sudden?"

"No one," he muttered. "Let's go. That is, if you're still going to Howler's. If not, we can just go home."

"I'm going to Howler's," I rushed to tell him.

Reaching his car, he opened the passenger door for me, but he stopped me before I could get in. "Look, Lyla. I gave Howler the chance to be with you in the past."

"Wait, what?" I shook my head, not understanding what he was saying. "What are you talking about?"

"Three years ago, when you decided you just had to go work with Barrick, I told him to do what he had to so you would stay. That included the two of you becoming a couple. I was fine with it if it meant you wouldn't leave."

My heart was pounding against my ribs so hard, I was surprised Judge couldn't hear it. "And?"

"And nothing," he said with a shrug of his massive shoulders. "He didn't choose you back then, Lyla. Just like he won't choose you now."

He didn't have to explain that to me.

I already knew that if it came down to it, Howler would let me go without a single moment of regret.

And I would be left broken and alone.

Just like always.

ten

Lyla

Howler was already home by the time Judge dropped me off.

Before I could even ring the doorbell, the door opened, and a seething blond giant stood over me.

"I told you to text me and I would pick you up."

I shrugged and walked past him into the house. "Judge showed up outside my class. He didn't leave me much choice."

The door slammed behind me, but I kept walking. In the kitchen, I opened the fridge and pulled out a bottle of water. The whole time, I kept my back to Howler, but I could feel his eyes on me. I could practically hear the wheels turning in his head as he tried to figure out what to say.

"What did you and Judge talk about?" he finally asked, and I closed my eyes.

"Ellianna's summer visit," I told him. Not a lie. We had discussed it.

"That's all?"

Opening my eyes, I turned to face him as I placed my water on the island. "Why? Is there something you don't want me to tell my brother?"

"No, of course not. I was just curious."

"I told him about us. I know he called you."

And I knew he hadn't been ready for that. I'd heard it in his voice, just as I saw it on his face now. My heart clenched painfully, and I turned away from him again. "Let's face it, Howler. This isn't going to work out. We both know it, so why are we even pretending otherwise?"

"No," he groaned, wrapping his arms around me from behind and locking me against his hard body. "No, Lyla. We will work. Just give us a chance, baby."

A single tear fell from my eyes, and I was thankful my back was to him. "If he makes you choose, you won't pick me," I whispered.

"You're wrong." He tried to deny it.

"You didn't pick me in the past, and you won't now." I covered his hands that were over my waist, stroking my fingertips over his scarred knuckles. "It's okay. I know where we stand. Let's just…enjoy this while we can. Okay?"

"Lyla," he breathed, his lips brushing over my ear before touching my neck. A delicious shiver went down my spine, and I leaned back into him. "Baby, I want to be with you."

"I want to be with you too," I answered honestly. But I wasn't stupid.

This wasn't going to have a happy ending for us.

But we could have a happy now, and that was enough for me.

At least that was the lie I kept telling myself as I wiped my eyes and turned to kiss Howler. He tried to say something more, but I didn't want to hear his empty promises. Not when we both knew the truth.

Keeping my lips on his to stop him from talking, I started tearing off his clothes. Who knew how long this would last? So I needed to make every moment I had him alone count.

When I got to his belt buckle, I finally pulled back. Panting, I carefully released the buckle then slowly lowered his zipper so I could reach in and wrap my fingers around him.

"Fuck," he groaned, pressing his forehead into mine. "Bed. We need a bed. Now."

Laughing, I released him and took off running. The sound of his feet pounding up the stairs behind me was my reward. No sooner had my feet touched the landing on the second floor than he was lifting me from behind without pausing and racing into his room.

We landed on the bed together, with me beneath him and his hands already tangled in my clothes, getting rid of every obstacle keeping us from becoming one.

And then he was inside me, his cock so deep, for a moment, I couldn't breathe.

"Fuck," he cursed savagely. "I forgot protection."

My nails bit into his sides. "Do you have a condom?" I panted.

"No. Don't keep them in the house, and I didn't stop at the store either."

"Guess we'll just chance it because I'm not letting you stop." I locked my legs around him. "Now shut up about the damn protection and just fuck me."

Grinning, he pumped his hips harder. "Yes, ma'am."

I felt ultrasensitive. "Are you bigger today than you were last night? Good God, man, you're huge," I moaned.

"Ah, poor baby. Are you sore?" He nuzzled my breast with his nose before kissing it.

"Not sore. Just… Ah fuck, that feels good." Humming my pleasure, I tried to remember what I was saying. "Just tender."

His thrusts changed, becoming gentle instead of rough like he'd been the night before. Every time he pushed into me and then carefully pulled back, I felt every inch of him. It was the most intense pleasure I'd ever felt in my life. My inner walls clamped down on him, hugging his girth and welcoming him inside, clinging to him when he would pull back.

"Better?" he murmured.

"It feels so good," I whimpered. "I don't want it to stop."

"Me either, baby. Being bare inside you is amazing." Sweat began to roll down his face and chest. "Maybe you can get on the pill, and we won't have to deal with condoms."

"O-okay. I'll do it tomorrow. Just don't stop doing what you're doing. Please, Howler."

"Baby, I couldn't stop now even if I wanted to," he said between gritted teeth, and I knew it was taking everything in him to hold himself back from taking me as hard as he had the night before. "Fuck, it was like this pussy was made just for me. Nothing has ever felt this good, Lyla. Fucking nothing."

I opened my mouth to tell him it was the same for me, but my orgasm snuck up on me. And the only thing that left my mouth was a cry of pleasure as my body began to shake.

Minutes later, he dropped his full weight on top of me, and I mewled my pleasure at having him there. "I love you so damn much, Lyla. We're together. Not just for now. For-fucking-ever," he rasped at my ear.

"Howler—"

"Say it," he ordered, lifting his head to meet my gaze. His eyes begged me to say the words.

"I don't—"

"Lyla!" he snapped. "Fucking say it."

"We're together…" He made a growling noise when I hesitated. "Forever," I whispered, wishing with everything in me that it was the truth.

eleven

Howler

Lyla was originally supposed to go to New York with her roommate, Mia, but when we found out Gwen had hurt Josie, Lyla had backed out so she could be with my daughter. Now that Josie was staying another night with my mom, that left us with an open Friday night.

Lyla wanted to go to the Underground, and I wasn't about to say no to her. Even if I did have to deal with Judge, I would give her what she wanted to make her happy.

As a Son of the Underground, I got to park behind the old warehouse where the fight was taking place that night. Judge owned them all, and I'd helped him convert them into Underground locations with a little help from my construction crews. What had started out as the occasional fight in Judge's basement when we were in high school had turned into a kind of cult following that was now the worst-kept secret in Northern Virginia.

I wasn't even completely sure why the fighters were called Sons of the Underground. It was just something Lyla had joked about one night before a fight when she was fifteen, and it stuck ever since.

Judge didn't fight much these days, but when he did, it was something the entire region came out for. And tonight was no exception. It was almost impossible to get to the warehouse with as many people as were already there. I honked my horn to get a group of girls out of my way and then drove around back to park close to the rear entrance.

"Let me get your door," I told Lyla as I opened my own.

"It's only a door," she muttered, yet she didn't move to open it herself. Grinning, I walked around the front of the SUV and opened her door.

Offering her my hand, I waited for her to place hers in it and then lifted it to my lips. "You look beautiful. Did you wear this for me?"

She glanced down at her red and black dress paired with knee-high black boots. They made her legs look even longer than they were. When she'd come downstairs wearing them earlier, I'd had to bite my knuckles to keep myself in check or I would have fucked her up against the wall then and there.

"I wore it for me, actually," she informed me, but that damn smirk on her luscious lips suggested otherwise.

As she stepped out, I put my arm around her, glancing around to make sure no one was following us. She still wasn't taking Gwen's buying a gun seriously, but I sure as hell was. My crazy ex was becoming unstable, and I was sure it was because of all the drugs she'd been using recently. If I'd known she was frequenting the drug dens, I wouldn't have even let her near Josie. The fact that she had been abusing my baby girl was driving me crazy.

Downtown was working the back door, making sure no one who wasn't supposed to be there got in. I got a chin lift from him, and he grumbled a greeting to Lyla as we passed.

"Who is he fighting tonight?" she asked me as we bypassed the locker room her brother was in and joined the crowd.

"No clue. Haven't talked to him today," I told her as we approached the bar. "But whoever it is, I feel sorry for the poor sonofabitch."

She pressed her lips into a tight line as she nodded. "He's been acting weird as hell, don't you think? And yesterday, it was like he saw a ghost, and then he just shut down and dropped me off at your house. After arguing with me that I should go home with him."

"Hell, baby, he's been acting crazy for a while. I don't know what his deal is." When we reached the bar, I ordered her one of her girly little fruity drinks with rum and a beer for me.

Tossing down the cash, I picked up our drinks, but her gaze was locked on something across the warehouse. "Babe?" I nudged her with my hand still holding her drink, but she didn't even blink. "Lyla?"

Shaking her head, she finally lifted her gaze to look at me. "I think I know what my brother's problem is." When she tilted her head in the direction she'd just been looking, I followed her line of sight.

"Ellianna? But I thought she went back to school." Mabel's daughter had spent the last three years at one of the most prestigious schools in the country. I'd never asked what she was studying, but I knew Judge had been footing the bill for her education.

He may be a total dick to Ellianna, but he loved Mabel like a mother. Hell, the woman had practically raised him before either Lyla or Ellianna had been born. All Mabel had had to do was say she didn't have the resources to pay for her daughter's expensive college degree, and Judge was pulling out his checkbook.

"Maybe she did go back to school," Lyla murmured distractedly. "Just locally."

"But why?" I took a sip of my beer, still holding Lyla's drink. "No offense, babe, but why would someone want to go to this school if they had a free ride to an Ivy League?"

"I guess that's something only Ellianna can answer." Turning, she walked away. I stood there for a moment, entranced by the sway of her hips in that dress.

Tipping up my beer, I swallowed the rest of the contents in two gulps and chucked the empty bottle in a nearby trash can before hurrying after my girl.

I reached her just as she and Ellianna were pulling back from each other, both of them laughing. "What the hell are you doing here?" Lyla wasted no time in demanding, a happy grin on her face.

Ellianna lifted a slender shoulder, her slightly upturned nose wrinkling a little. "Why does everyone keep asking me that?" the other woman muttered. "Can't a girl get homesick and want to be closer to her family?"

Lyla crossed her arms over her chest. Staring her friend down, she waited. After only a few seconds, Ellianna tossed her long blond hair over her shoulder and huffed. "I got tired of being Zachary Bennet's charity case. I'm home because it's just cheaper for me to study locally."

"How are you Judge's charity case?" Lyla demanded. "He's an ass, but I've never seen him treat you like that. Did he say something to you? I swear, I'll kick his ass—"

"Lyla, I love you, but don't get in the middle of this. Just leave it alone." Giving her another hug, Ellianna stepped back. "I'm here with my roommates, so I need to get back to them before the fight starts."

"You realize Judge is the one fighting tonight, right?" Lyla called after her.

Ellianna turned with a gasp, her face losing all color. "But he never fights anymore."

"Rarely," she agreed. "Call me, Elli. We seriously need to catch up."

Swallowing hard, the blonde nodded before walking back to her friends. I watched as she stopped in front of a group of three other girls, all of them about her age, maybe a little older. Even from where I was standing, I could tell Ellianna looked physically ill all of a sudden.

"I can't believe she's been here all this time and I haven't seen her until now," Lyla complained as she finally took her drink from my hand. "And seriously, why would she think she is Judge's charity case? He must have run his mouth. I swear, he's a great man until he gets near Ellianna, and then he turns into the worst kind of bully."

I kept my mouth shut while she finished her drink, but my eyes drifted back to Ellianna several times. She was a few months older than Lyla but looked younger. The twenty-one-year-old barely looked eighteen. She was slender, hardly any curve to her body at all, with the longest, shiniest blond hair I'd ever seen. Her facial features had an almost otherworldly quality to them, like one of those fairies or elves in the fantasy movies I could never get into, no matter how good the cast was.

The girl was beautiful, I would admit that, but her beauty was different from Lyla's. Ellianna was fragile, delicate-looking, as if she needed someone to protect her from the world. Lyla had an aura about her that screamed badass woman who could take on the world and win.

Judge normally went more for women of the latter type, but I could almost understand the appeal of someone like Ellianna. A guy's instinct was to protect those weaker than himself. He would want to protect and take care of Ellianna, but he wouldn't want to *want* her.

Maybe he was fighting himself on everything with the girl. Whenever my best friend was conflicted, he didn't handle that shit well.

When Lyla's drink was empty, I took the plastic cup from her and tossed it into the trash before pulling her into my arms and lowering my head. Brushing my lips over her sweet, fruit-flavored mouth, I completely forgot about Judge and Ellianna and the world in general.

Lyla fisted her hands in my shirt, holding on as I deepened the kiss right there in front of everyone. “Wh-what was that for?” she panted when I lifted my head.

“No reason other than I couldn’t help myself.” Kissing the tip of her nose, I nodded my head toward her roped-off VIP area. “Fight’s about to start. You ready to sit?”

Licking her lips, she nodded, and I linked my fingers through hers as we walked over to the area Judge always left open just for his sister.

We’d barely sat down before the lights were turned low and the first fighter was being announced. Lyla snapped her head up, and our gazes locked as we both grimaced. “Sledge,” she groaned. “He’s fighting Sledge.”

I dropped my arm around her shoulders, cursing inwardly. Sledge was a mean sonofabitch. No one ever wanted to fight him simply because he was a dirty motherfucker.

If Barrick hadn’t been busy, he probably would have been the one to ref. Instead, a nervous-looking official stepped into the cage behind Sledge as he bounced around, hyping up the crowd, getting boos so loud, the windows shook.

Then Judge’s name was announced, and the entire building was suddenly trembling with the screams of the crowd. But Judge didn't even seem to notice them as he walked purposefully out of the back and straight into the ring. As the cage doors closed behind him and the lights came back on, he locked his eyes on someone behind Sledge, and I watched my best friend's entire face twist in agony for a single heartbeat before he shut down his emotions.

Sledge shifted, and I saw who had caught Judge's attention.

Ellianna.

twelve

Lyla

Holding my breath, I watched as Judge tore his gaze off Ellianna.

If I hadn't been watching them both so closely during their brief exchange, I would have missed the look of pure torment on my childhood friend's beautiful face. But when I looked at my brother again, it was to find his face totally emotionless. Which was completely unlike it had been only a moment before, when he'd looked at Ellianna like his life was flashing right before his eyes.

I may not have been able to read what he was thinking right then, but this fight told me plenty. That it was Sledge in the cage with him spoke even louder.

It told me that Judge wanted to cause someone pain, but with his choice of opponent, it said he wanted to bring the pain on himself just as much as he wanted to dish it out. And with Sledge, that was exactly what he would get.

An inch shorter than my brother, Sledge made up for the small difference in height with the muscles that caused his body, which had been bean-pole-like in high school, to swell like the fucking Hulk. He'd graduated a few years ahead of me, and he'd left for two years immediately after. He'd returned looking like he'd spent the time in a cult that worshiped the steroid gods.

Roids were strictly forbidden in the Underground, but by the time he came back, they must have been out of Sledge's system because he'd passed the piss test he was required to take to become a Son—and, as far as I knew, every test since.

Judge was not lacking in the muscle department, not when his freaking legs looked like tree trunks and his arms and back were roped with corded muscles that trembled with every step, every inhale, he took. But his muscles had been acquired the old-fashioned way, unlike his opponent's.

Sledge, who was perhaps the dirtiest Son in the entire Underground, landed the first blow. It was a sucker punch, striking the side of my brother's head before the ref had even indicated the fight could begin. Sledge's fists were like anvils, and the blow had Judge misstepping before he turned on the other man.

With a roar, he tackled Sledge, taking him to the ground. With his arms trapped, Sledge was defenseless to protect himself against the blows to his ribs, kidneys, even his liver.

A smirk lifted my lips as my brother tore Sledge apart right in front of my eyes. This was my world, the one I'd grown up in, the one I'd been homesick for from the first day I'd walked away for the job my cousin had given me. I thrived on the emotions the crowd projected into the warehouse. The screams, the boos, the cheers, and the shouts of profanity. All of it filled my soul with something it longed for whenever I was off on another assignment.

Without even realizing it, I leaped to my feet, screaming and cheering on Judge right along with the rest of the crowd.

Out of nowhere, Judge's head flew back, blood pouring from his nose. Sledge had an open wound on his forehead, but it was all too obvious he'd headbutted my brother. He didn't even seem fazed by it, whereas Judge stumbled to his feet, trying to clear his head.

It was all the opening the other man needed. Jumping to his feet like his entire body didn't ache from the beating he'd been taking, Sledge hit Judge in the face with an uppercut that had my own head snapping back with the force of it.

Shaking his head to clear it, Judge's eyes landed on Ellianna, directly to his right. Her pale blue eyes were wide, her face a sickly green. I watched her mouth his name, his real name, and a single tear trickled down her cheek.

Something he saw on her face seemed to snap him out of his dazed state, and just as Sledge was coming in for a hit that would have surely knocked my brother out, he ducked. When he came up, he landed a direct blow to the side of the other man's head. Sledge went limp, falling at Judge's feet with a thud that echoed through the warehouse.

While the ref attended to the downed man, I took stock of my brother. He had a gash across his nose that was bleeding, as was his left nostril. There was a bruise already forming on his jaw, and with the way he kept running his tongue over his teeth, I suspected one or two of his back teeth were loose.

Other than that, he looked fine, but I knew he would need to be looked over by the doctor to rule out a concussion or any other internal injuries.

From across the cage, I saw Ellianna jump to her feet and rush toward the exit. Judge took two steps, as if he were going to follow, then stopped and turned his back to the sight of her running away.

"Did I actually see what I thought I saw?" Howler muttered from beside me as I sat down.

"That my brother is crazy in love with Ellianna?" He nodded and I grimaced. "Do all guys treat the woman they love but don't want to love like total shit?"

A heavy sigh left him, and he dropped an arm around my shoulders. "It's a defense mechanism, baby."

"Sounds like they're just pussies to me."

"That too," he agreed with an amused twist of his mouth. "But we learn our lessons eventually."

An indelicate snort left me. "I'll have to take your word on that," I told him snarkily, while hoping he was right. I wouldn't ever say Howler had been a bully like Judge was to Ellianna, but he'd definitely put my heart through the wringer more than a few times.

Grasping me by the hips, he lifted me up and onto his lap. The back of my neck began to prickle, and I didn't have to look to know every eye in the building was suddenly on us. Instead of glancing around, I melted into him.

Straddling his waist, I kissed him slowly. Lifting my head long moments later, I brushed my nose against his. "Let's get out of here," I purred.

His Adam's apple bobbing, he nodded. "Best idea I've heard all night, baby."

Grinning, I stood. As I turned, Judge caught my gaze, his brows lifted. *Let him do whatever he wants*, I thought as I smirked at him and lifted my hand to give him a finger wave, before letting Howler pull me through the crowd toward the exit.

***

Dawn was just breaking through the window when I heard Howler's phone ring. Groaning, he unwrapped one arm from around me and blindly reached for it. "Yeah?" he rasped, still half asleep.

But a moment later, I felt every muscle in his body tense, and he released me completely as he sat up on the edge of the bed. “Yeah, okay. I’ll be there as soon as I can.”

Turning onto my side, I watched him stand and walk toward the closet. “Something’s wrong?”

“Just a little issue at one of the sites, baby. I’ll go take care of it and hopefully be back before lunch.” Pulling on a pair of boxer briefs, he grabbed a pair of jeans. Once they were fastened, he picked out a plain white T-shirt and walked back to the bed without putting it on.

Leaning down, he kissed me, slowly and leisurely. “I’ll be back soon.”

Yawning, I nodded, snuggling deeper into the pillow that smelled like him. “Be careful. Love you.”

I felt his lips on my shoulder, and he whispered, “Love you, Lyla,” before the bed shifted as he straightened.

I closed my eyes, waiting for the door to shut behind him before releasing the breath I’d been holding. It had taken everything in me not to beg him to blow off whatever needed his personal attention and ask him to stay in bed with me until it was time for Josie to get home.

After the night before, openly defying my brother by kissing Howler in front of the entire Underground and walking out with him afterward, I could sense our time together was coming to an end. Like a bomb timer ticking down, I could feel almost hear the tick-tock of the clock running out.

Soon, Judge would make Howler choose. I'd seen it in his eyes as I'd smirked at my brother on our way out and pretended I didn't have a worry in the world. Like I didn't already know what Howler's choice would be when his best friend gave him the ultimatum that would destroy me completely.

Knowing I wouldn't be going back to sleep, I grabbed my iPad off the nightstand and pulled up the app to watch one of my favorite K-dramas. But even as the hot Korean actor was making the unsuspecting love interest fall for him, my mind kept drifting.

After having to rewind the same scene three times and still not retaining a single word they were saying, I tossed the iPad away in disgust with myself and went to shower. When I was done, I tossed on a pair of running shorts and a hoodie before going down to the kitchen.

Cherie was supposed to bring Josie home at noon, so I still had hours of alone time. Dropping my phone on the dock on the kitchen counter, I selected a playlist and got to work.

Growing up, Mabel had taught me how to cook right along with Ellianna, and it was one of my favorite things to do. Especially when there was a lot on my mind and I just wanted to turn it off.

Howler had someone come in and clean three times a week, and they stocked the fridge and pantry for the most part. Fresh veggies were in the crisper, so I pulled out what I needed and got to work on a pasta salad that both Howler and Josie would enjoy for lunch.

While I was at it, I made some homemade yeast rolls we could use for sandwiches, something father and daughter always devoured whenever I'd happened to make them in the past. They loved my cooking, no matter what I made for them, and I loved taking care of both of them.

To go with it, I made a cookie cake and the homemade icing Josie loved so much, but I didn't decorate it. She would want to help me, so I put everything aside for her to turn the dessert into her own masterpiece once she was home.

By the time everything was finished and the kitchen was once again spotless, it was time for Josie to get home. Hearing a vehicle pull up in the driveway, I bounced through the house and opened the front door just as Josie came running up the walkway.

Seeing me standing there, she threw herself into my arms with a happy squeal. “I missed you!” she announced, clinging to my neck. “I was scared you wouldn’t be here when I got home.”

I kissed her cheek, holding her tight as I smiled at Cherie, who was walking toward us with Josie’s backpack in hand. “I’m not going anywhere anytime soon,” I told her, silently praying I wasn’t lying to her.

“What is that divine smell?” Cherie asked as she entered the house.

“I’ve been cooking. Are you hungry? I’m sure the pasta salad is chilled by now.”

The older woman shook her head. “I’m actually on my way to lunch with a friend, but thank you, darling.”

I smirked at her. “Who is this friend?”

Cheeks turning pink, she tapped me playfully on the arm. “None of that, young lady.” Placing the backpack on the couch, she returned to the door. “You two be good.”

Laughing, I waved to her as she walked to her vehicle, before turning back to my favorite person in the world. “Should we wait for Daddy to get home from work before we eat our lunch?”

She nodded as we walked into the kitchen. “Daddy doesn’t work on Saturdays, though.”

“He had an emergency,” I explained.

“Cookie cake!” she exclaimed when she saw the now completely cooled huge cookie sitting on the island waiting on her. “Can I have some, Lyla? Please, please, please?”

“This is our dessert tonight, kiddo,” I informed her as I helped her up into the chair so she could see the cookie better. “But you can decorate it however you want with the icing I made.”

Once her hands were washed, I let her get to work on decorating.

By the time she was done, it was almost one o’clock, and Howler still wasn’t home. Grabbing my phone, I called him to see if everything was okay.

"Hey baby," he answered in his deep voice. "Looks like I'm going to be here a little longer than expected. Go ahead and eat without me."

"Have you eaten today?" I asked, concerned.

"Grabbed a biscuit on my way to the site this morning."

Rolling my eyes, I started pulling out the makings for the sandwiches I'd planned on being our lunch. "Very healthy."

"I was in a hurry, babe."

"Which site are you at? Josie and I are bringing you something to eat that isn't soaked in saturated fat and grease." Hearing me, Josie clapped her hands happily, and I winked at her.

"That really isn't necessary," he started, but I wasn't having any of that bullshit.

"Howler," I said his name, warning dripping from my tone, and with a sigh, he told me where he was. "We will see you in less than an hour," I told him, and I disconnected before he could complain.

With Josie's help, I made enough sandwiches to feed the three of us and packed us each an individual serving container of pasta salad. Grabbing drinks and putting an entire pot of coffee into the thermos I found, we walked out of the house just as Judge's town car pulled into the driveway to pick us up.

At the construction site, it appeared they were in the early stages of building someone's house. With the bag containing our lunch in one hand and holding Josie's with the other, I carefully walked to the edge of the site and waited, knowing that unless we had a hard hat on, Howler would lose his mind if either of us set foot inside, where it was so dangerous.

Spotting us, Howler left his foreman and jogged over to us. Scooping Josie up into his arms for a kiss, he threw his arm around my shoulder and kissed my cheek. "What have my girls been up to?"

"Daddy, we made you lunch," Josie told her father excitedly. "And tonight, we get to eat the cookie cake I decorated. It's so pretty. I put flowers all, all, all over it." As she spoke, she widened her arms more and more, making her father laugh.

"She's not exaggerating," I assured him as we walked toward the little trailer that was one of the temporary offices for each job site. “I think there is more icing than cookie.”

“That’s my favorite way to eat a cookie cake,” Howler said with a grin.

“Mine too!” Josie exclaimed happily.

In the trailer, he set his daughter down, and I walked over to one of the two desks to unload our food. When I passed him the thermos, he groaned his appreciation. “You’re the best,” he muttered, kissing the side of my head. “I’ve been dying for some coffee.”

Hiding my smirk, I placed the food in front of him and Josie before grabbing my own. Producing plastic forks from the bag, I sat down beside Josie and opened my pasta salad container.

“Babe,” Howler moaned around his bite of sandwich. “How did I ever survive without you all these years? This sandwich tastes like heaven.”

Heart leaping with happiness, I dug into my meal without responding.

Thankfully, Josie gave us a play-by-play of her sleepover at her grandmother’s house, keeping us both distracted while we ate.

Once we’d finished and all the containers were empty, I started packing everything away.

"Will you be home for dinner?" I asked, only to clamp my lips together when I realized I sounded like a nagging wife.

"I shouldn't be here much longer. Now that I've been fed some of the best food this side of the country, I think I can figure out the issue and get the show on the road." Standing, he kissed me. When he pulled back, his lips twitched with amusement. "So yes, I'll definitely be home for dinner. What are we having?"

"Cookie cake for dessert!" Josie informed him proudly.

"I hadn't given dinner much thought. What would you like?" I allowed myself to stroke my hands down his chest once before stepping back. "Josie and I can stop at the grocery store on the way home if we don't have what you want."

"You are all I want," he breathed close to my ear before brushing his lips against my neck. I shivered but forced myself to take another step away from him. It would be hard to explain to Josie why I was walking funny if I continued to let her father make my panties soaking wet.

"Roasted chicken it is, then," I told him, and Josie cheered.

"I love Lyla's chicken."

Howler smiled for his daughter. "Me too, baby girl."

He walked us out to my brother's car, where Tony was still waiting. As we approached, the driver's window lowered, and Howler bent to speak to the man before telling him to stop at the grocery store on the way back to his place.

Straightening, he ruffled Josie's hair, then kissed my lips one more time. "Thank you for lunch."

"My pleasure," I murmured, brushing a speck of dark lint off his white shirt. "We'll get out of your way now, Daddy."

His nostrils flared. "We have to talk about you calling me 'Daddy.'"

I lifted my brows. "You don't like it? Is it creepy?"

"No, baby. It does things I can't tell you about in front of my kid." Tapping me on the ass, he opened the back door of the town car. "Buckle up, and don't do anything reckless. I'll see you in a few hours."

"Yes, Daddy," I said with a wink and buckled Josie into her booster seat.

Jaw clenching, he shook his head at me. “You’ll pay for that later, Lyla.”

“Looking forward to it.”

thirteen

Lyla

I was just getting Josie out of the bathtub when my phone rang.

Unsure why it was ringing, I looked at the noisy thing apprehensively, an uneasy feeling settling in my gut.

Wrapping the towel around Josie's wet little body, I urged her toward her bedroom. "Go on, Jo. I'll answer this and be right there."

"Okay," she singsonged and skipped away.

Finally looking at the screen to see who was calling, I realized it was Barrick and lifted it to my ear. "How did your meeting go last night?" I asked by way of hello, knowing the meeting that had been planned for weeks with Mia's father had been weighing heavily on him.

"Where are you?" he demanded, sounding…off. There was a strain in his voice, desperation, and something more. If I didn't know any better, I would have thought my hard-ass cousin was close to tears.

"I'm at Howler's."

"I'm in fucking Georgetown, and I have no way back. Mia left, with Braxton, and they took my Jeep. No taxi or Uber will take me that far, and I'm about to lose my fucking mind, Lyla."

"Wait, wait. Hold up. What do you mean, Mia and Braxton took your Jeep? They're supposed to be in New York for the weekend." The dread I'd first felt at the sound of my phone doubled, because he wasn't making any sense to me. "What the hell is going on, Barrick?"

"Mia found out," he said with a groan. "She knows everything."

"Shit," I muttered. "I'm assuming she didn't take the news very well, then?"

"That's an understatement. Her uncle called the cousin yesterday to check in on his daughter, and Mia happened to pick up, and she heard me in the background. She showed up at the hotel this morning with Braxton and her mother, and things went south rapidly."

"Oh man. I've heard stories about Mia's mom."

"Lyla, they're all true. She handled those four Demons like they were fucking toddlers. She had one of the brothers by the ear and was pulling him around like a kid instead of a grown man. And he just let her. It was surreal." He blew out a frustrated breath. "But it's Mia who scared the hell out of me. She wouldn't believe me when I told her I love her. Please, Lyla, send the car. I have to get back to campus and fix this before I lose her."

"Okay, okay. I'll call for the car now. I'm coming with you, though. She might listen to me." I hoped, at least.

"Thank you," he rasped just before the phone went silent.

Texting the driver who was always at my disposal, I walked into Josie's room. "Jo-Jo, I have to go out for a little while."

"Will you come back?" she asked, her eyes filling with sadness.

I crouched down in front of her, giving her a reassuring smile. "Of course I will. It will probably be late before I get back, though, so don't give your dad a hard time about going to sleep. Okay?"

"Okay." She gave me a tight hug, then handed me the brush. "Will you braid my hair before you go?"

I made quick work of her hair, then hurried downstairs where Howler was sitting on the couch in the living room. He glanced up as I grabbed my purse. "Where do you think you're going?" he demanded as he got to his feet and followed me to the door.

"I have to go pick up Barrick. Shit hit the fan, and Mia now knows that we're her secret security detail." Opening the door, I leaned up and kissed his lips. "I'll probably be late getting back. Don't wait up."

"Lyla, wait." I paused on the threshold, waiting. "Just be careful, okay."

I kissed him again. "I promise." With a wave, I ran down the driveway just as Tony pulled up. "Love you."

The drive to get Barrick felt like it took a hundred times longer than the drive back to campus. He kept scrubbing at his beard, cursing himself for not having told Mia, for even agreeing to the job in the first place. I understood completely.

If I'd known how much Mia would come to mean to me, I never would have taken the job either. Guilt that I'd been lying to her had been eating at me since that first week of school. She'd become a great friend, and all I'd done was keep secrets from her the whole time.

It wasn't like this with every job Barrick and I worked together. Sometimes the girl we were protecting found out and didn't give a damn about it. Other times, they never found out. But either way, we'd never been emotionally involved with any of them the way the three of us had been with Mia.

She was different from any other job we'd worked. She wasn't spoiled, even though her family had more money than God. She didn't constantly complain or play the poor-pitiful-me card at the drop of every hat because she'd fucked up her leg and the dance career she'd always envisioned for herself was over. She was strong and sweet with a whole lot of feisty tossed in. She loved with her full heart and made those closest to her feel like they truly mattered.

Not one of the girls in the past was anything like Mia. They whined if they so much as chipped the nail polish on their expensive manicure, blamed the world for every little problem that inconvenienced them in even the most minor of ways. And work was something they'd never even thought about a day in their lives. Kindness for them came with a steep price tag, and having a backbone in the face of their moneymakers was laughable.

I'd never lost a wink of sleep when working previous jobs, but with Mia, I'd been tormented by thoughts of how she would react should she ever find out our friendship had started out with her dad hiring Seller's Security to keep her under constant surveillance.

As we stepped onto the floor of the dorm that I'd shared with Mia for the starting week of the term, the first thing I saw was half a dozen freshmen standing around, whispering. Right in front of our room, box upon box of my things was already littering the hall.

"Shit," I muttered to Barrick as we moved past the gawking freshmen. "I didn't think she would be pissed at me."

At least not to the point that she was actually kicking me out of our dorm room. It wasn't like we'd lived together other than that first week of the semester since she'd been staying with Barrick practically from the moment they met. But until this past week, I'd been staying in the dorm. I'd kind of liked it, except for the bitchy RA on the floor.

Mia walked out of our room, yet another box of my things in her arms. Eyes red-rimmed and swollen from crying, she spotted me and threw down the box like it had personally insulted her.

"I trusted you. I thought you were my friend," she cried angrily.

My heart clenched at the hurt and sadness in her eyes just below her justifiable rage. "Mia," I tried to soothe, "we are friends. Just because I was guarding you doesn't mean we aren't friends."

"You lied to me," she whispered brokenly, and her pain became my own. I wanted to wrap my arms around her and hold her. She was the little sister I'd never had and didn't even realize I needed until she came into my life. "I don't want you here. I figured since you didn't want to be here to begin with, you could either move in with your brother or stay with Howler."

"Mia—" I started to plead with her to listen, but Barrick interrupted.

"You live with me."

"I live here." Ice coated her voice, making me shiver at the coldness coming from her normally warm personality. "Braxton went to get my things."

"No way. He can just take them back." He started to grab for her, but she backed away and walked into our room.

With a groan that sounded like it was being torn from him, Barrick followed, only to have the door slammed in his face. "Mia! Open the door. We have to talk."

"Go away, or I'm calling security," she threatened.

"I am the fucking security! Now, open the door before I break it down."

Angrily, she jerked the door open, her green eyes flashing fire at him as her nostrils flared. "You are not my security any longer, asshole. Take yourself and your backstabbing cousin, and get lost. I don't want to see either one of you."

The elevator opened down the hall, and I glanced over the freshmen's heads to find Braxton walking our way with a huge suitcase in one hand and a box in the other.

"Take it back," Barrick snarled, and I tensed, fearing for the safety of my younger cousin for a moment.

"Nope. Sorry, but you aren't calling the shots anymore."

While the two of them stood there having a stare down, I tried to get through to her. "Mia, I'm sorry. I didn't mean to hurt you like this. It started off as a job, I admit that, but after that first week, I really liked and cared about you. We *are* friends, I swear to you."

"What's going on here, people?"

Cursing under my breath, I moved into Ruby's path. Fuck, but I hated the RA. She was on a real power trip because she thought she was the governor of our floor or some shit. No one liked her, but only Mia and I had ever called her out on her abuse of power, so she was constantly calling me a bitch. "This is a private matter, Ruby. We don't need you putting your big nose in it."

"This is my floor, Bennet. It's my job to ensure all my girls are safe. And Little Miss

Goody-Two-Shoes here doesn't seem particularly safe from the looks of it."

"Fuck off, Ruby," Mia tossed over her shoulder as she walked back into her room. "I'm not in the mood for your bullshit today."

"You're never around, so I assumed you had dropped out," Ruby goaded as she leaned back against the wall close to Braxton. I wasn't surprised when she started eye-fucking Braxton, any more than I was that he point-blank ignored her.

"You mean you stopped sucking cock long enough to notice I wasn't around?" Mia gasped in mock shock and stuck her head out the door, eyeing Ruby dispassionately. I had to bite my lip to keep from laughing, because I knew it wouldn't win me any points with my friend if I did. "Bitch, please. I have enough on my plate right now. I don't need your bullshit on top of it. Get lost."

"If you're sticking around, make sure you follow all the floor and dorm rules," Ruby muttered, knowing she wasn't going to win this round. "That means no overnight guests of the opposite sex."

“Not a problem, trust me,” Mia said with a dry laugh as she started to close the door in Barrick’s face yet again.

My older cousin stopped it and pushed his way inside before closing and locking the door behind them.

Releasing a heavy sigh, I leaned back against the wall, unsure what to do now. First, I needed to get my things moved, though, I guessed.

“Don’t suppose you’ll help me get this shit downstairs?” I asked Braxton, who was just standing there in the middle of the hall, looking about as unsure of what to do as I felt.

“Let me make sure Mia is okay, and I’ll help you,” he promised after a moment. “She’s taking this worse than I feared, Lyla.”

The defeat in his voice made my heart constrict, and I hugged him. “I know. But she’ll come around. She’s mad right now, and yeah, hurt because we kept this from her, but she won’t stay mad forever.”

I hoped.

fourteen

Howler

It was late and I was in bed when Lyla got home. I hadn't even tried to sleep, knowing I wouldn't get any rest as long as she wasn't in bed with me. Less than a week with her sleeping in my arms and I was already addicted to it.

I knew something was wrong as soon as she walked into our bedroom. Dejectedly, she started pulling off her clothes, and without so much as looking my way, she went into the bathroom.

Hearing the shower start, I tossed back the blanket and climbed out of bed. She was just standing beside the shower, her hand in the water to test the temperature, her shoulders drooped as if she had the weight of the world pressing down on them.

"Things didn't go well?"

"She kicked me out of our room. Braxton helped me store all my things at Judge's. That's why I'm covered in sweat." Turning to face me, I saw the tears glazing her eyes that she refused to let fall.

Lyla wasn't a crier, so I knew this was hurting her.

"She broke up with Barrick, and she doesn't want to see me. She said..." Sucking in a deep breath, she lowered her head. "She said I was a backstabbing liar."

"Ah, babe." Crossing to her, I pulled her into my arms. She hugged me back as tight as she could, as if she were afraid I'd let her go, and buried her face in my bare chest.

"She's right. I did lie to her." Her voice was barely a whisper and so full of sadness, it broke my heart.

Grasping her chin between my thumb and forefinger, I tilted her head up so she had to meet my eyes. "You were doing your job, Lyla. If you could have told her, you would have. I know she means a lot to you, and I'm so sorry you're hurting right now, baby. But she will come around. Just give her a little time."

Her teeth sank into her bottom lip, and she gave a small nod. Brushing a kiss over her lips, I reluctantly released her. "Shower, and I'll make you a snack."

Downstairs, I made her a sandwich, but I didn't know just how hungry she was, so I grabbed a slice of the cookie cake as well as a glass of milk. Putting them on a tray, I carried them back upstairs. As I walked into the bedroom, I heard the shower turn off, and I put everything at the end of the bed.

When she walked out, wrapped in a towel and making my mouth water as my own hunger began to gnaw low in my gut, she looked like she was feeling a little better.

Giving me a sad smile, she walked over to the closet where her luggage was and bent to pull out a pair of panties.

I clenched my jaw as I watched her. Fuck, but she was so damn beautiful. Rubbing my hand over my mouth, I shifted restlessly. "How about tomorrow I make room for you to hang your clothes up in the closet? There's space for another dresser too. I could build you one if you tell me how big you want it."

She grabbed a shirt out of my closet, one of my old T-shirts, and pulled it over her head before letting the towel drop to the floor. Turning to face me, she pinched her brow together. "Are you sure about that? I'm okay living out of the case."

"I want your stuff touching my stuff," I told her. Maybe it sounded lame, but I didn't care. It was the truth. "I want you to move in permanently, Lyla."

Her pretty eyes widened. "Really?" I nodded, holding my breath as I waited for her to answer. "Judge won't like me living with you full time, Howler."

"Fuck Judge," I growled. "He has nothing to do with you and me, baby. It's our choice. Your choice. Please, move in with me."

Sighing, she walked over to the bed where I was still standing and wrapped her arms around my waist. "Can I think about it?"

It wasn't the "yes" I was hoping for, but it wasn't the "no" I'd been dreading either. "Take all the time you need, babe." Kissing the tip of her nose, I turned her around to show her the small feast I'd made for her. "Get comfortable. You can eat in bed while we watch some TV and cuddle."

That earned me a true smile, and she hopped up onto our bed. I placed the tray on her lap then crawled in beside her with the remote in hand. She curled up against me, offering me a bite of her sandwich. I shook my head, wanting her to eat every bite I'd made just for her.

"I'll get my late-night snack when you're done," I promised with a wink that had her eyes dilating with need.

"I could get used to this," she muttered. Pink filled her cheeks, and I wondered if maybe she hadn't meant to say that out loud.

Grinning, I didn't call her out on it and tell her to just move in if she liked it so much. Instead, I found us something to watch and soaked up the feeling of the world—*my* world—finally being right.

***

Having spent more time making love to Lyla than sleeping the past several nights had made me miss out on rest. After she'd fallen on top of me the night before, we'd both passed out.

Only to have Josie wake us up by jumping on the bed the next morning. I barely lifted my head, making sure we were both covered with blankets before I let my head drop heavily back onto my pillow.

"I want pancakes," Josie chanted as she bounced between us. "I want pancakes."

Laughing, Lyla caught her around the waist and pulled her down between us, kissing every part of her little face. "Pancakes, huh?"

Giggling, Josie nodded her little blond head. "Can I help you make them? Please, Lyla? I'm a good helper."

"I don't know. What do you think, Daddy?"

What I thought was I fucking loved it when she called me "Daddy." And not just because she could make it sound dirty as hell at times. When she called me "Daddy," I got this image in my head of Lyla pregnant with our baby, while Josie and a few other kids ran around her feet. All of them calling her "Mommy."

"I like bananas and chocolate chips in my pancakes," I grumbled sleepily instead. "Think you can handle that, Jo?"

"Yes!"

Lyla sighed dramatically. "Okay, okay. Jo-Jo, you go down and make sure we have enough bananas. Do not, I repeat, do not touch the stove."

"Yes, ma'am." Josie hopped down, and her little feet took off running before they even hit the floor.

After giving me a quick kiss, Lyla jumped up, grabbing clothes as she rushed after my kid. Lifting my head, I grinned at the sight of her sexy ass disappearing out the door seconds before it closed behind her.

Groaning, I sat up and tossed my legs over the side of the bed. I could have slept another four hours at least, but there was no way I was going to miss out on the fun of watching my girls making pancakes together.

Rushing through a shower, I walked downstairs still pulling a fresh shirt on over my head. The smell of bacon was already filling the air, and I heard Lyla telling Josie to get ready to catch the first batch of pancakes when I walked into the kitchen.

"Daddy," Josie called out, holding a plate with two pancakes already on it. "We're making your favorite."

Walking up behind Lyla, I kissed her shoulder. "Smells good, ladies. What can I do to help?"

"Juice?" Lyla suggested distractedly. "And set the table."

After kissing her again, I got to work. With all the amazing food Lyla had been filling my stomach with the past few days, I was going to have to hit the gym harder than ever. But I wasn't going to complain about it. I would happily kill myself doing cardio if it meant more moments like this with her.

As I set the table, I watched the two girls together. Lyla was patiently showing Josie how to flip a pancake. Josie's tongue stuck out in concentration as she used both hands on the spatula to flip the small pancake. It landed almost perfectly, and Lyla beamed her pride in my little girl.

"Great job, Jo!" she cheered. "Now, how about adding more chocolate chips to this one and those sliced bananas?"

"Okay," she agreed enthusiastically as she climbed back into her chair at the island and did as instructed.

"Howler, could you get the bacon before it burns?" Lyla called out as she poured more batter into the pan.

"On it, babe." Grabbing a pair of tongs, I took the bacon out of the skillet and put it on the paper towel-lined plate already waiting. After stuffing a piece into my mouth, I carried the plate to the table and started pouring us each a glass of orange juice.

Once all the pancakes were done, Lyla and Josie joined me at the table.

Taking a hungry bite of one covered in chocolate chips and fresh bananas, I groaned my pleasure as the taste exploded on my tongue. "Girls, you have made Daddy very happy this morning."

Josie giggled, and Lyla grinned as she gave me a wink. For the next ten minutes, no one talked much as we enjoyed our breakfast.

But as I was shoving my last bite of bacon into my mouth, licking syrup off my thumb as I did, my phone went off. Glancing down at the screen, I saw it was Judge and bit back a curse.

For a second, I considered just letting it go to voice mail, but I knew if my best friend was calling this early on a Sunday morning, something was up. Wiping my mouth, I stood. "I have to take this. But don't touch the dishes, babe. I'll take care of it as soon as I'm done with this call."

"It's not a problem," she started to protest, but I kissed her to shut her up.

"I'll clean up. You and Josie go relax when you're done eating." Hitting connect, I lifted the phone to my ear. "What's up, man?"

"You sound too awake and chipper for nine o'clock on a Sunday morning," Judge groused.

"Just had breakfast with my two favorite girls," I told him as I entered my office at the back of the house and shut the door. "Why are you up this early?"

"Man, I haven't even been to bed yet. I haven't slept in days…I think. Fuck, I don't even know at this point." Blowing out a harsh exhale, he got to the point of his call. "Just wanted to warn you two of my people will be camped in your driveway from here on out. On a whim, I had someone pay a visit to Gwen's apartment yesterday. She wasn't home, but what they found there was enough to make me uneasy. Honestly, I thought she was just blowing smoke when she bought the gun and started making threats against Lyla. But… Hell, I'll send you the full report I got. Just don't let my sister out of your sight, and if you do happen to have to, make sure my people are with her."

Breakfast was suddenly sitting heavy in my gut, and I sat down behind my desk. "Email me everything you have. I want to see it now."

No sooner did I have my computer screen on than I got the email. Clicking on it, I saw a picture of a handwritten report as well as pictures taken around Gwen's apartment.

The first thing that caught my eye was the drug paraphernalia lying on the coffee table that was littered with garbage and dirty dishes, all of it right on top of Josie's coloring book and crayons. Fuck. Did my baby girl have to see and be around that kind of dangerous shit whenever she was with her mother?

The next photo showed the couch and a box of shells that was open. Bullets were spread across the cushions, two magazine cartridges right beside them. One was full, the other empty. Did she get extra magazines to go with the gun when she bought it, or did she get them from someone else, I wondered as I clicked through the other pictures.

That crazy bitch really wanted to hurt Lyla. But I'd die before I let that happen.

"Howler?" Judge grunted my name, reminding me he was still on the phone.

"Yeah, I'm here. Just looking at these damn pictures. Do you think she had the drug shit around Josie?"

"Yeah, man. I'm sorry, but I do," he told me honestly. "She's a selfish bitch, Howl. It wouldn't have mattered to her that her kid was playing around things that were potentially deadly for her."

"Can you have her arrested for this? I mean, fuck, Judge. Josie's little coloring book is right there beside what looks like a crack pipe." I scrubbed my hand through my hair, tugging at the roots.

"I'm doing my best, but even my pull will only go so far. She no longer has custodial rights, so Josie will be just fine for now. But it wouldn't hurt anything if both you and Lyla got restraining orders against Gwen. Lyla, especially."

"We can do that first thing tomorrow," I assured him. "And then I'm taking her to work with me."

"Good idea. Keep her close. As long as Lyla isn't on her own, hopefully Gwen won't chance getting near her." I heard him yawn. "I have to go. Maybe I'll actually get to sleep now."

"Maybe you need to clear your conscience," I suggested. "Call Ellianna and tell her you're sorry for being a total douche."

"Fuck off," Judge growled seconds before the phone went silent in my ear.

Dropping my phone on my desk, I went through the pictures in front of me again. Every time I saw the drugs and that damn coloring book, I wanted to kill Gwen with my bare hands. Then my eyes would be drawn to the bullets and the full magazine cartridge, and my rage only doubled.

No one was going to threaten my woman.

fifteen

Lyla

"If you think for two seconds I believe you, then you've lost your fucking mind," I snarled at the supplier in front of me.

I'd given in somewhat gracefully that morning when Howler had asked me to come into work with him to help out in the office. He may have been balls deep inside me at the time and withholding my orgasm until I agreed, but I wasn't about to tell that to anyone else.

All morning, I'd worked alongside Cherie, but then she got called out to pick up one of her other grandchildren from school because one of Howler's sisters was stuck at work and couldn't do it herself. Before she left, Cherie told me she had a meeting with one of their suppliers who'd become later and later with their shipments, as well as shorting them. But she trusted me to deal with him.

When the fortysomething man arrived, I'd taken one look at him and nearly laughed. He looked his age and then some, but he dressed like a frat boy with the collar of his polo pulled up and his hair overly gelled to the point a hurricane couldn't have budged it.

He walked into the office with a swagger. When his eyes landed on me, he licked his lips and ran his thumb over them, and I felt dirty just letting his eyes roam over me.

But I'd put a smile on my face and shook his hand, offering him something to drink as I took him into the conference room for our meeting. I listened patiently to his explanation about why his drivers were continually late with deliveries and why we were shorted a little more every time.

His assurance that he oversaw every order and loaded it personally was bullshit. I had our copies of the order slips in the binder Cherie had given me before she left, showing what was ordered, and they sure as hell didn't match up to the papers he offered as proof. It couldn't have taken much for him to have written a new order slip, tossed the customer's copy, and said it was our mistake, not his.

Which brought us to the point where I lost it and called him out on his shit.

"Now, listen, sweetheart—"

I slapped my hand down hard on the conference table, the sound so loud it echoed around the room. "I am not your goddamn sweetheart. Or 'sugar' or 'honey.' My name is Miss Bennet, you sexist motherfucker. And as of this afternoon, our contract with you expires. Which was probably the only reason you got off your lazy ass and came here in the first place. Bronson Construction will no longer be needing your services as we've already got a new supplier." I stood, tossing his documents in his direction, smirking when they hit him in the face. "Have a good day, douchebag."

"Now, listen here, bitch," he snapped as he grabbed my arm hard.

I reacted on instinct. Countering his hold, I folded his arm behind him and shoved his face into the table, hard. His head bounced off the thick wood, making him shout in pain even as he struggled against my grip. I twisted my elbow into his back, making him curse me.

"Now, you listen, bitch," I tossed his words back at him. "You ever touch me again, I will make you eat your own dick. I said we no longer need your services. I suggest you get the fuck out of this office and crawl back into the hole you climbed out of this morning."

A knock on the glass wall overlooking the rest of the office had me turning my head. Howler stood on the other side, his hand lifted after knocking on the glass, his eyes narrowed.

I gave him my sweetest smile and blew him a kiss.

Sighing, he walked over to the door and entered the room. "What the fuck, Lyla?"

"He grabbed me," I told him with a casual shrug and finally released the asshole.

Howler's face twisted with rage. He got in the supplier's face, his voice deceptively calm when he spoke. "You put your hands on my woman?"

The man swallowed nervously. "I-I apologize."

Howler jerked him closer by his raised collar. "Not to me. To her." Turning the man around, Howler made him face me. "Apologize to the lady. Now."

Sweat was beading at the supplier's temples and on his upper lip, his face pasty white as his throat bobbed convulsively. "I-I'm so sorry, Miss…Bennet."

"Whatever. You're not worth my time. Just get out before he does something he will regret." I picked up the binders Cherie had given me earlier and walked to the door. "Don't do anything that will get you arrested," I tossed at Howler over my shoulder.

There was a lot of work that still needed to be done, so I concentrated on it rather than wondering what Howler did with the creep supplier.

I kind of liked taking care of the office. It was continuously busy, and the day passed quickly.

So busy, that I didn't even see Howler until it was time to leave to pick up Josie. Grabbing my coat and handbag, I started for the door just as he came out of his office.

"Ready?" he asked, tucking a rolled-up set of plans under his arm.

I frowned as he came closer. "You're finished for the day? I was just about to go get Jo-Jo."

"All done. Just going to take this home with me and finish it up tonight after Josie goes to bed." Grasping my hand, he linked our fingers.

As we walked outside, I noticed him glancing around, but I didn't call him out on it. Something must have spooked him, because Howler was never nervous like that. I bit my tongue until we were in the vehicle and he'd pulled into traffic, and then I confronted him.

"Want to tell me what the hell is going on?"

He glanced my way for a second before turning his attention back on the road. "What do you mean, babe?"

"I mean you seemed like you were waiting for someone to jump out of the bushes and ambush us back there. And I know for a fact that you are normally in the office on Mondays until six. At the earliest. I could easily pick up Jo and take her home."

He shrugged, keeping his eyes trained on the horizon. "Maybe I wanted to spend the entire evening with my girls."

"Ah, how sweet. Now tell me what the fuck is really going on." His jaw clenched, a pulse beginning to tick in his jaw, and I knew it was something serious if he was going to remain mute. "Okay. Then what the hell are you doing driving in the opposite direction of the preschool?"

“Gotta make a quick stop. Judge needs you to sign something, and then we can pick up our Josie.”

Damn, I liked how he said “our Josie” like she was mine just as much as she was his. I liked it so much that I shut up for the rest of the drive to my brother’s office.

In the cage, Judge was so named because he was the judge, jury, and executioner. What he said was law, and if the Sons or even the fans who came to watch the fights didn’t follow the rules, then he was the one who dished out the punishment.

When he was twenty-five, he became the youngest judge in the state. Having graduated from college and then law school at an early age, he’d more than gotten his four years of experience before being offered the judgeship. Now he was one of the richest and most influential men under thirty in the country.

His secretary greeted both Howler and me with a grim smile while she was on the phone. With a wave of her hand, she indicated we could go into his office. Howler nodded his thanks, and with his hand at the small of my back, guided me toward the closed door.

My brother was standing by the window overlooking the back courtyard, but when the door opened, he snapped his head around as if annoyed at the intrusion into his privacy. Seeing us, however, he relaxed his expression, and he left his place at the window to greet me with a hug.

"How was your day?" he asked me, but I had a weird feeling he was actually asking Howler how my day went.

Stepping back from him, I glanced from one man to the other. "Howler said you have something you need me to sign?"

"Yes, it's right here." Walking to his desk, he pulled out a stack of documents and flipped to the last page. "Just need your signature here and here, and it will be taken care of."

He offered me a pen, but I wasn't stupid. He'd taught me from an early age never to sign something I hadn't read first. And as much as I loved him, I didn't trust him very much at that moment.

"Very funny," I said, snatching up the documents and flipping back to the first page. "What the hell?" I tossed the papers onto his desk and turned to confront both men. “Why am I signing a restraining order?”

“Just covering all the bases with this Gwen thing,” Judge said with a casual shrug.

Crossing my arms over my chest, I lifted my brow at him, but when I got only a stony glare back, I turned it on Howler.

“We have reason to believe Gwen isn’t just blowing smoke about her threats to shoot you,” he confessed. “Judge’s people found magazine cartridges in her apartment. Multiple ones, with plenty of bullets to take out you and a dozen other people.”

I couldn’t believe they were letting that stupid bitch scare them. “I broke her wrist. Even if she did happen to have the balls to try to shoot me, she couldn’t handle a gun very well. I’m not scared of her, and I’m not signing that stupid restraining order. If I do, it just proves to her I’m nervous. And I’m fucking not.”

“Gwen is psychotic, Lyla,” Judge tried to reason. “And her wrist will make her that much more dangerous. What if she comes after you and Josie is with you? What will you do if she shoots at you and hits Josie by mistake?”

I felt all the blood draining from my face. The world began to spin for a moment, and if Howler hadn't wrapped his arms around me, I knew I would have fallen on my ass right then. Just the thought of something happening to my precious little Jo-Jo was enough to make me almost pass out.

"Easy, baby," he murmured near my ear. "It's okay."

"Sign the restraining order, Lyla," Judge commanded. "If not for your own sake, then for Josie's."

Turning my head, I pressed my face into Howler's chest and breathed in deeply in an attempt to ground myself. Judge was right. I needed to sign the order so I could protect Josie.

I felt Howler kiss the top of my head, and I blew out a heavy sigh before pulling away and walking back to Judge's desk. I picked up the pen and the paperwork. Flipping to the last page, I signed the two places already indicated for my signature and tossed the pen aside.

"Anything else?" I choked out past the lump in my throat.

“Howler, this one is yours. Sign it, and the two of you will be covered.” Judge produced another restraining order, already typed out, and offered both it and a pen to Howler.

After signing it, Howler took my hand. Lifting it to his mouth, he kissed my palm. “You did the right thing, babe.”

I could only nod, still shaken by the idea of something happening to Josie.

sixteen

Lyla

Josie was bouncing off the walls as we walked into Cora's School of Performing Arts Tuesday evening.

Barrick was already sitting in the waiting room, surrounded by mothers and daughters. More than a few of the mommies were sending my cousin covert looks of interest, but the majority of them were out of his age range. He didn't go for cougars, unlike a few of the other Sons, and even if he did, he was so in love with Mia, he didn't see anyone else.

"Hey," he greeted as I sat beside him, his voice raspy from disuse.

"Hey." I gave him a sympathetic smile. "She still not talking to you?"

"No. And now she's talking about going back to California after this semester." He leaned his head back against the wall behind his seat and glared up at the ceiling. "I told her, if that's what she really wants, then I'll find us a place out there and have us moved in before the spring term starts. And she fucking killed me by saying she wants UCLA but she doesn't want me."

I gave his arm a squeeze, hating that he was hurting. "She's just mad right now. Give her a little time, Barrick. She loves you."

Tormented dark eyes met mine. "I know that and she knows that, but she won't say the words. And it's killing me Lyla."

"Miss Mia! Miss Mia!" Josie pulled our attention to her as she ran toward Mia when she came out of a room down the hall. "I'm ready to dance."

Mia gave her a kind smile. "So am I, sweet girl. And I have a surprise for you."

"You do? What is it?" Josie demanded excitedly.

Mia laughed softly. "You'll just have to be patient and wait for the other girls to arrive before I make an announcement. Go on. I'll be right in. I just have to grab my phone so I can get the music."

Knowing this was likely my only chance to talk to her, I stood and walked toward her just as she turned away. "Mia." I waited for her to turn back. “Could we have coffee tomorrow? I really would like to talk to you.”

“No thanks.” Her voice was so cold, it could have frozen over the Bahamas. “If you will excuse me.”

Frustrated, I said the first thing that came to mind. “So, you can forgive Braxton, but not me? That doesn’t seem fair if you ask me.”

Her laugh was dry and humorless. “Life isn’t fair, Lyla. Haven’t you realized that by now?”

Without so much as another look at me, she turned and walked away, disappearing into what I thought was the dance instructors’ locker room.

Damn it! My heart was hurting because she wouldn’t give me the chance to apologize. She’d forgiven Braxton like it was nothing, but me, she wouldn’t even talk to.

Feeling slightly defeated, I walked back over to my cousin and flopped down inelegantly into the chair beside him.

“Still think she will forgive us in time?”

I shook my head. “I have to. Otherwise, I think my heart will actually break if she doesn’t.”

“Mine’s already fucking broken,” he muttered.

We both sat there silently for the rest of the time while Josie was in class. When she came out, humming what sounded like a Christmas song and talking nonstop about Sugar Plum Fairies, I was thankful for the distraction.

Mia didn't come out of her classroom, so I gathered all of Josie's things, told Barrick goodbye, and we left.

My town car was waiting right in front of the dance studio, but I was still vigilant as I walked with Josie close to my side. Ever since Judge had hammered home for me that Josie could be in danger, I'd taken the whole Gwen thing more seriously.

If something were to happen to Josie, there would be no place for the bitch to hide, though. I would personally make sure of that.

"Will you come watch me in the recital, Lyla?" Josie asked once she was buckled into her booster seat and we were on our way home.

"Of course I will," I assured her. "I can't wait to watch you be the best little Sugar Plum Fairy ever."

I thought that would make her happy, but she got a worried look on her face. "Do you think my mommy will come?"

"I…" Pausing, I took a deep breath. "Do you want her to, Jo?"

That got me an adamant headshake. "No! I don't want to see my mommy. Please, don't make me."

Stroking a hand over her hair, I tried to give her my best smile. "Then you won't have to, baby girl. Your daddy and I will make sure you won't ever have to see her again."

Her shoulders dropped with relief. "Are you and Daddy dating?" she surprised me by asking suddenly.

"I… Maybe? Is that okay?"

She nodded enthusiastically. "Will you and Daddy get married?"

I felt sweat mist my forehead and upper lip. Shit, this kid asked all the hard questions. "Are you hungry? Let's have a quick dinner tonight."

The good thing about children Josie's age, they were easily distracted. "Can we make grilled cheese?"

"Sounds good." I would have agreed to anything if it stopped the line of questioning that was making me edgy.

But more than that, it reminded me that a future like that wasn't in the cards for Howler and me. I was just happy to take what time we could get together. With Judge's head stuck on Ellianna, we had a reprieve, but I knew it was only a matter of time before he made his best friend choose.

Howler still wasn't home when the driver dropped us off—and stayed in the driveway to watch the house. I fed Josie then helped her with her bath before tucking her into bed.

As I turned off the light in Josie's room, I heard Howler downstairs, and I went down to see if he was hungry.

Walking into the kitchen, I expected to see Howler, but the room was empty. Figuring he was just in his office, I backtracked and knocked on his office door before sticking my head in the room. "Hey, are you…hungry?"

The light was on, but the room was empty. Other than the window that overlooked the backyard, the door was the only way into the room, and the window was closed. I hadn't seen Howler in any other room, and I would have if he were home.

A feeling of unease began to stir in my gut, and I found myself running back upstairs to Josie's room as I called Howler.

"Hey," he greeted after two rings. "Sorry I'm late, babe. The client wanted three more rooms added to the plans, and we had to figure that out before I could leave. I'm on the road right now and should be home in fifteen minutes or so."

"Howler," I whispered, walking into Josie's room and checking every inch of it to make sure no one had gone in there while I was downstairs. "I heard someone downstairs a few minutes ago. I thought it was you. I went into your office to ask if you wanted something to eat, and the light was on."

"Fuck. Is the guard in the driveway?"

"I don't know. I was more worried about checking on Jo."

Opening the closet door, I was relieved to find it empty. Turning back to the bed, I knelt down so I could look underneath.

"Her room is empty." I sat on my rear, leaning my head back against the bed. "If there was someone in the house, I think they were only in your office. They probably heard me and ran off."

"I'll be there in five minutes. Lock yourself in Josie's room and don't come out until I get you." Before I could respond, the line went silent.

Grimacing, I stood and went back to the door. Locking it, I turned off the light I'd switched on when I first entered the room, which surprisingly, hadn't woken Josie, and moved to the window. There were a few lights in the backyard, and I tried to see if there was anyone out there. But all I saw were shadows, and nothing moved, not even the wind blowing the tree branches.

Maybe I just thought I heard someone downstairs.

But that didn't explain the light on in Howler's office. Judge's security was parked in the driveway, but that didn't mean someone hadn't walked through the backyard. The locks had been changed the day after Howler thought Gwen had been in the house, but maybe the office window hadn't been locked.

No, I quickly told myself. Howler checked the windows in each room every single night before bed.

"Lyla!"

I didn't even want to think about how many laws he'd broken to get home as quickly as he did, but I was just thankful he'd gotten here in one piece. Unlocking the door, I opened it and was engulfed in a bone-crushing hug.

"Are you okay?" he choked out, his arms finally releasing their vise-like hold so he could skim his hands over every inch of my upper body.

"I'm fine," I assured him. "Nothing happened. Maybe… I don't know. Maybe I just thought I heard someone downstairs."

"No. You didn't. Tony wasn't in the car in the driveway when I pulled in. He must have seen something."

From the bed, Josie made a grumpy noise. Releasing me, Howler walked over to look down at his daughter. Bending, he kissed her forehead and tucked the covers up over her more securely.

As he straightened, his eyes met mine. "Stay here. I'm going to call Judge and the cops. I'd feel better if you were here with Josie."

"Of course. I won't leave her."

His lips tilted up ever so slightly. "Thanks, baby." As he walked to the door, he paused long enough to brush a soft kiss over my lips. “I’ll be back up as soon as I can. Go ahead and get comfortable. This may take a while.”

seventeen

Howler

This shit was getting old fast. This was twice Gwen had gotten into my house, twice my girls had been put in danger by that bitch.

The rage that was burning through my veins was making my head throb.

Judge and five of his security team were in my kitchen, along with three police officers. After the cops had inspected the entire house, they determined there had been no forced entry, but I was sure Lyla was correct. Even though she second-guessed herself about hearing someone downstairs, I knew she must have.

Tony had seen someone walking around the side of the house and run after them, but he'd lost them two blocks later. From the height and build he described, it had to be Gwen.

But how she'd gotten into the house, and why she'd been in my office, were both unanswered questions. Nothing had been misplaced. Other than a few papers out of order in the top drawer of my desk, there wasn't really anything to tell me anyone other than I had been in the room. It was like she was a fucking ghost the way she got in and out and then disappeared so easily when Tony was chasing her.

Or she had someone helping her.

But who would be stupid enough to help her when they knew I would kill them if anything happened to my little family? Whether people accepted it or not, Lyla was a part of my family. She was mine, and I would always protect what was mine.

"Let's get security cameras put in on all sides of the house," Judge told his men. "I want them up and running by morning."

With a nod, they filed out of the kitchen to get it done. After we spoke to the cops one more time, they left as well, promising to have patrolmen driving the neighborhood every hour.

When we were alone, Judge leaned back against the counter, his massive arms crossed over his chest. "We can't prove it, but Gwen broke the restraining order. If we could show it, then the cops could arrest her. Which is another reason to have security cameras installed. Maybe we should talk about the girls moving in with me until she is no longer an issue."

I clenched my jaw, hating the very thought of Lyla and Josie leaving my house, but I knew he was right. They would be safer at his place. There was more security, and he lived in a gated community.

But before I could so much as nod in agreement, Lyla spoke from behind me. "I'm not leaving."

"Lyla—" Judge started in a beseeching voice, but she was already shaking her head.

"No," she snapped angrily. "I'm not running away and hiding behind my brother from this crazy cunt. Bump up the security, put in the cameras. Do whatever else you have to, but I am not running away."

"He's right, Lyla," I attempted to reason, even as my gut clenched painfully.

Hurt flashed in her eyes, but she clenched her jaw. "No."

"Think about Josie," Judge tried again.

"I am thinking about Jo." Crossing her arms over her chest just as her brother was doing, she glared him down. "I'm showing her that she should never run away. Even when the boogeyman is her own goddamn mother."

"Stop being so fucking stubborn, Lyla!" Judge shouted, losing his temper. "Your life is at risk here. She has a gun. Do we know if she can actually handle it? No, but do you really want to chance your life to find out?"

"The only way I'm leaving is if Howler tells me he doesn't want me here," she told him, not even sparing me a glance. "I can and will take care of myself. And Josie too. Keeping Gwen out is your job. Fucking do it."

If she thought I would ever want her to leave, she was crazy. Hell, I didn't even want her or Josie to go to Judge's place. It burned and caused a dull ache in the region of my heart to send them there when it was my job to protect them both until my dying breath. But that was exactly what having them stay with him would be. Protecting them.

"Howler, tell her," Judge tossed at me.

"No."

My answer had them both looking at me with surprise, but it was Lyla's expression that made me want to punch something. Preferably myself for making her doubt her place in my life. Sometimes, it was like Lyla thought we had a timetable and it was quickly running out. But I'd be damned if I ever let her go.

Josie and I both needed her too much for me to lose her now. I didn't care what I had to give up to keep her, but she was ours and I wouldn't let her slip through my fingers again.

"You look confused, Judge. Let me clarify. Fuck. No. Lyla stays as long as she wants. I'm not telling her to go because I'm not going to lie to her and tell her I don't want her here. She belongs here. This is her home."

"You…you really mean that?" she whispered, taking a hesitant step toward me.

I grabbed for her before I lost my mind with all the distance between us. "Of course I fucking mean it. I love you, Lyla."

"I thought—" She broke off, shaking her head even as she threw her arms around my neck. "It doesn't matter what I thought. I'm just so happy you didn't tell me to go."

"You two are a real pain in the ass, you know that?" Judge grumbled. "Fine. Have it your way,

Lyla. I'll make this place as secure as fucking Fort Knox."

Her arms only tightened around me. Realizing his sister was done talking to him, he muttered a curse and pushed away from the counter. "Guess I'll get to work, then. Try to calm your shit down, Lyla."

"Try to change your dickhead attitude, Judge," she called after him without turning around. "Maybe then Ellianna could possibly stand to be in the same room with you for more than two seconds."

She couldn't see him, so she missed the way his entire body seemed to turn to stone. His face tensed, and he opened his mouth to blast her, but our eyes locked before a single world left him. I shook my head, giving him a look that told my best friend he would regret it.

I knew Lyla ran her mouth, and sometimes she was definitely a bitch, but I loved her, and I wasn't about to let anyone disrespect her. Not even her damn brother.

He stomped through the house, and I barely heard the front door slam shut behind him on his way out. As soon as he was gone, the kitchen felt calmer, and Lyla began to relax.

Tilting her head back, she smiled as she looked up at me through those thick as hell lashes. "You said this is my home?"

"Fuck yeah, it's your home, baby. Right here beside me and Josie is where you belong from here on out." Brushing the hair back from her face, I touched my lips to hers in a kiss that barely skimmed over her mouth but had her gasping nonetheless. The sound was like a shot of pure lust straight to my cock. "You're ours, Lyla."

Tears filled her eyes, her smile trembling as she shook her head at me. "That's all I've ever really wanted. You and Jo, that's all I need. Nothing else matters."

"Thank fuck," I growled, kissing her again. This one was deeper, more demanding, so she wouldn't run her mouth when I lifted my head and told her point-blank, "Now we can move your shit in here."

Dazedly, she lifted her brows. "Did you honestly think I would say no to that?" Grasping my shoulders, she used them as leverage as she jumped up and wrapped her legs around me.

"Judge has this. Let's take a shower," she purred at my ear before sinking her teeth into my neck.

Fighting myself not to back her against the fridge and fuck her right there, I grabbed her ass and sprinted through the house. As I took the stairs two at a time, she giggled against my flesh.

"Fucking killing me," I muttered as I walked through our bedroom and kicked open the bathroom door.

With her still in my arms, I turned on the shower to let it warm up before carrying her to the sink and sitting her on the edge. Her fingers were already working on the buttons of my blue button-up, a small growl leaving her when the fourth one got stuck.

Pulling back, I ripped the shirt apart, causing the rest of the buttons to go flying around the room. Her teeth sank into her bottom lip as her eyes skimmed over me hungrily. Tossing the shirt aside, I started on the rest of my clothes, afraid if I undressed her, I would hurt her in my need to touch her soft skin.

"Get naked," I commanded, and her giggle as she started pulling off her clothes was music to my ears.

By the time I had my boxer briefs down, she was standing there completely bare. I paused, taking in the sight of my woman. She was so damn beautiful with her long dark hair falling over her shoulders, her soulful eyes brushing over me like she couldn't stop herself from looking at what belonged to her.

Realizing that she was really there, that she was mine and moving in with me, was too much to take in. Getting everything I'd ever wanted had my legs going weak. I dropped to my knees before her and pressed my lips to the soft skin just below her navel.

Her fingers combed through my hair before cupping the back of my head and holding me to her. "Howler," she murmured. "You're trembling."

"Just taking all of this in, baby. I love you so goddamn much it hurts to breathe right now. Give me a minute."

She stroked her fingers down my neck as she dropped to her knees in front of me. Her lips brushed over mine, a gentle kiss that made my eyes close in sweet agony. I wrapped my arms around her tiny waist, pulling her closer, needing all of her pressed into me.

But when her teeth nipped my bottom lip, I lost it. With a savage curse, I dragged her to the floor. Cupping her pussy, I felt how wet she was, and there was no saving her from what was coming.

Thrusting deep, I didn't give her time to adjust before I was pounding into her. Her nails scratched down my back, marking me as I tried to imprint the shape of my cock inside her.

"Ah fuck," she whimpered. "You feel so good. Please don't stop."

"Couldn't, even if I wanted to," I panted. "Hold on to me, baby. Hold as tight as you can."

"Harder," she begged, amping me up. "Please, harder."

"Fuck. Grab your knees, Lyla. I need to go deeper." Sweat was already rolling down my face and back. "Goddamn, baby, your pussy is so wet. Are you going to come for me so soon?"

Her pussy clamped down around me, proving to me how right I was. Her back arched, her hips pushing up into me as I thrust so hard into her, I saw stars as I came deep inside her.

It was several minutes before I could get my breathing under control. Groaning, I pulled free from the tightness of her body and got to my feet. Bending, I lifted her and carried her into the shower that had filled the entire bathroom with steam.

A content moan left her as I lathered her hair, massaging her scalp as she leaned limply against me.

“We have to stop having sex without a condom for a little while,” she muttered sleepily. “I haven’t started the pill yet, and if you’re not careful, Josie is going to get a little brother or sister.”

I hid my grin as I continued to wash her hair. “You say that like it’s a bad thing, babe.”

Fighting a yawn, she pressed her forehead to my chest as I started massaging her neck. “I don’t think you’re ready to be a daddy again.”

Carefully, I tilted her head back into the spray to rinse her hair. “Lyla, with you, I’m ready for anything.”

eighteen

Lyla

By the end of the week, we were all on edge. There'd been no sign of Gwen, not even at the drug dens. Judge had all eyes looking out for any sign of her, but it was like the woman really was a ghost.

My brother was true to his word and turned Howler's house into a fortress. Howler's office had an entire wall of screens dedicated to all the security cameras surrounding the house. There wasn't just a driver sitting in the driveway, but four different members of Judge's personal security walking the perimeter of the property at any given minute.

And classes, well, I'd given up on those for the rest of the week and emailed all my professors to tell them I had a family emergency come up. Instead, I went to work with Howler every morning. When Josie didn't have school, she came with us, and I spent the days running the office and watching over her.

Cherie was practically bouncing around the place with me helping her out, and she left early every day. Her son hadn't been wrong when he'd told me she wanted to retire, and I was sure she thought I was going to take over for her full time.

The idea wasn't without appeal. I enjoyed the work more than what I'd been doing with Barrick.

I wasn't hiding anything or sneaking around behind anyone's back, babysitting people I couldn't stand. Everyone in the office seemed to like me, and I got to spend more time with both Howler and Josie throughout the day. And with Howler having chosen me and telling my brother to basically fuck off, then asking me to move in—more like commanding it, but I was going to pretend like he'd asked—I was considering the job position more and more.

"We're leaving early," Howler announced as he came out of his office, minus any building plans, for once.

I looked down at my desk overflowing with a hundred things that needed my attention before I could leave. We still had three hours before we normally left, so I hadn't worried about getting it done. "I have a lot to do."

"So, we can come in tomorrow and work half a day." Wrapping his arms around me, he slid his hands down over my ass and pulled me in for a quick kiss. "But we're leaving now. Barrick just called me and said he's fighting tonight. Needs to blow off some steam in the cage."

Spending a little time at the Underground did sound like fun, and I was always ready to support my cousin when he was fighting. "What about Jo?" I asked, worried about her.

"Mom already picked her up. Judge sent two of his men with her, and they will be spending the night at her house." Kissing the tip of my nose, he slapped both his hands across my ass and stepped back. "Now, come on, woman. I want to feed you before the fight."

Sighing dramatically, I grabbed my things off my desk and put my hand in his.

As we walked out to the SUV, we both glanced around for any sign of Gwen or anyone else who might try anything. This whole thing had made me paranoid as hell, and I was getting fed up with it all.

Once we were on the road heading home, I began to relax a little.

"We're kid-free for the weekend, baby." Clasping my hand as he drove, he lifted it to his lips, kissing our linked fingers. "What do you want to do?"

"I need to do a little shopping." Mia's birthday was on Monday, and even though she was still pissed at me, I wanted to give her something. Maybe it would help break the ice and get my friend to forgive me.

I missed her.

With Mia, I didn't have to pretend to be something I wasn't. She'd accepted me as I was—and even liked my K-drama shows. She was the closest thing I had to a best friend besides Howler, and I didn't want to lose her.

"Okay. Whatever you want, babe."

"You don't have to come with me—" I started to tell him, but he shot me a look that had my mouth snapping shut.

"Where you go, I go. Don't argue with me on this, Lyla."

"Okay," I said with a shrug.

His eyes widened before he switched them back to the road. “Are you feeling all right?”

“I’m fine, why?”

“Because you aren’t running your mouth,” he grumbled.

“Why would I run it when I want you to go with me?” I asked, brows lifted.

That seemed to make him relax. “Because you like to drive me crazy.”

I grinned wickedly at him. “Howler, the only place I want to drive you crazy now is in bed. And if you hurry, I can do just that before we go to the Underground tonight.”

His answer was to punch his foot down on the gas, making me laugh happily.

***

Braxton was already waiting in my VIP area when we got to the Underground later that night. He sat slouched in his chair, glaring off into space, and I knew it was a bad day for him.

Howler took one look at him and put himself between my cousin and me. I rolled my eyes and pushed him out of my way so I could sit beside Braxton. "You okay?"

"She's here," he muttered. "With some guy."

"Who?" I asked, curious as to who could have put that pained look on his face. I'd cunt-punch whoever did that to him.

"Mia. She brought some douchebag with her."

Shit. I glanced around quickly and, after a moment, spotted Mia as she sat down with a leanly muscled guy who was so freaking good-looking, I had to blink a few times to make sure I wasn't seeing things.

Dark hair styled in an unkempt way that looked like he didn't care, dark eyes, and a bone structure that must have been chiseled by the gods themselves. Even with the distance I was from him, I could tell his clothes were top-notch quality and expensive.

He leaned in to talk to Mia, who didn't shy away but leaned back into him, just as comfortable with him as she'd been with both Braxton and Barrick. The look in her eyes spoke of affection, maybe even love, and all I could think was, "How can she do this to Barrick?"

He'd screwed up, but that didn't mean Mia should grab the first dick that pointed itself her way and then wave him in front of my cousin like a red flag. Because that was exactly what it was going to be like when Barrick saw her with this guy. The Beast would turn into a raging bull.

As if feeling our eyes on her, Mia turned her head and looked right at us. After a moment, she clenched her jaw and looked away, pretending like we weren't even there.

The guy beside her wasn't even looking our way. He draped his arm over her shoulders, as if he had every right in the world to touch her, and pulled her in close to say something in her ear.

Whatever he said had a grin tilting her lips as she shook her head at him. Her lips moved, but I couldn't read them. The guy's face grew serious, and I saw something akin to longing in his eyes that made me want to jump up and snatch Mia away from him before Barrick saw them.

I didn't want my cousin to be hurt any more than I wanted to have to testify at his murder trial. Both were likely to happen, however, and I glanced around to make sure he wasn't close by.

Just as I was taking a deep breath, relieved Barrick wasn't anywhere he could see his girl with someone else, the lights went out and Ridge was being announced.

"Fuck, Howler," I groaned as the crowd booed the other fighter. "Please tell me you didn't know he was fighting this asshole."

"I didn't know, babe," he assured me, a muscle ticking in his jaw as he clenched and unclenched his teeth. "Stay the hell in your seat, no matter what happens. Hear me?"

"Then you better intervene if it comes to it," I told him, crossing my arms over my chest as I looked back at Ridge, who had his eyes on Mia.

Ridge wasn't a dirty fighter, but he was mean as hell and there were rumors he liked to hurt women. If Judge'd had proof, he wouldn't have allowed Ridge to be a Son, so I didn't know if it was true or not. But the way he was looking at my friend right then turned my stomach.

Her date wasn't a complete tool, though, shifting so his body was protecting Mia from any possible danger. Not that it would have done much good if Ridge really were out to take Mia away from him. Ridge's fists were like anvils. One punch from them and the guy would have been out cold before he knew what was coming.

Once Ridge was in the cage, Barrick was announced. The Beast walked out, his usual swagger gone as he marched toward the cage with purpose in his dark eyes.

"Why the fuck is he wearing a shirt?" I asked Braxton.

"Got some ink earlier," he said with a shrug.

"I'm sorry, what?" I demanded, blinking at him in surprise. "Barrick got a tattoo?"

"Yup."

"The same guy who screamed like he was being tortured when he got a flu shot when he was fifteen?"

"Yup."

I still wasn't convinced we were talking about the right person. "The same guy who, at the age of twenty, passed out when he had to have blood work because he was practically hyperventilating over being stuck with a little needle? That Barrick?"

"Yes, Lyla," Braxton bit out. "It took two hours. The piece takes up a lot of his chest and has some pretty sick detail to it."

"Well, what did he get?" I half shouted when he didn't say anything else.

"A firecracker exploding."

Well, fuck. That was why Barrick had faced his fears and gotten the ink. He must have been missing Mia more than I imagined if he'd been willing to sit and let someone tattoo his nickname for her onto him.

I looked back to where he was about to enter the cage just as his eyes landed on Mia. I could actually see the tension leaving his muscles until his gaze shifted and he finally spotted her date. His head snapped back like he'd already taken a blow to the face from Ridge, making him stumble as the cage door closed behind him.

Even in the dim light, I saw tears fill Mia's eyes before her date turned her head so she would look at him.

I held my breath, waiting for the match to start, terrified for Beast now. He was one of the best fighters in the Underground. I would have put him on the same level as both Judge and Howler, but this distraction would have his attention on Mia and not on the fight—where it needed to be one hundred percent focused on Ridge.

He was so focused on Mia, he didn't even see Ridge coming up behind him. Before I could yell to alert him, Mia's cry of distress had him turning.

A single punch to the jaw had Ridge collapsing, his entire body becoming dead weight as he lost consciousness.

"Always knew that pussy had a glass jaw," Howler said with a grunt beside me.

I would have laughed if I weren't still watching Mia and Barrick. No sooner was Ridge counted out then Barrick was out of the cage and carrying Mia back to the locker room.

Around us, everyone else was on their feet, moving into groups to talk about their disappointment in the night's fight. Beside me, Braxton shifted, but I put a hand on his arm before he could stand.

"Don't." I knew what he was planning even before he'd moved.

"Just going to the bathroom, Lyla. Fuck. Let a guy piss."

I stood, causing Howler to as well. "Right. So, you weren't going to go over there and deal with Mia's date? Show him the error of his ways for going out with your best friend's girl?"

"My cousin's girl," he corrected. "Mia is my best friend. And I just want to talk to the guy."

"What he means, babe, is he wants to kill the fucker," Howler interpreted. "Should I help him bury the body, or keep him where he is?"

"For now, let's not let him commit murder," I said with a smirk.

nineteen

Howler

Shopping was the at the bottom of my list of fun things to do, but Lyla seemed to be having a good time as I followed her from one store to the next, carrying the heavy bags she acquired in every single one of them she walked into.

She'd told me that morning over breakfast that she was only looking for something for Mia's birthday. Six stores later, we hadn't found anything for Mia yet, but Josie now had a brand-new wardrobe and a handful of new toys. We also had new sheets, towels, and an air fryer.

I wasn't complaining, though. My girl was having fun, and I was happy to carry all her shit around the mall for her.

"I need a new bra," she announced as Victoria's Secret came into view.

My entire body went hard, picturing her in that store trying on all those sexy-as-fuck bras. "Let's go, then," I told her, rearranging the bags in my hands so I could put a hand at the small of her back and urge her in.

Laughing, she led the way. The store was dimly lit and chilly, giving the place the kind of mood lighting that made me want to push Lyla into one of the changing rooms and fuck her against the door.

At least ten other women were in the store, but none of them paid us much attention as Lyla walked around, browsing all the bra styles on the mannequins.

"What color, do you think?" Lyla asked as she fingered one of the bras hanging beside a mannequin modeling a bra with straps crisscrossing over its tits.

"I like the light pink," I told her honestly after looking at all the color options hanging up.

"Me too." She flipped through the rack until she found her size and pulled it off, before bending to find her size in the matching panties. When she straightened, she headed for the checkout counter.

"Babe," I whined. "I thought you were going to try it on."

Laughing, she switched direction, heading to the back where the fitting rooms where. A saleswoman was back there measuring other women, and she unlocked one of the doors for Lyla. “Let me know if you need anything,” she said with a grim smile.

As Lyla walked into the small fitting room, I pushed in behind her. “Howler,” she complained. “There’s no room.”

“Baby, I’ll make the damn room—even if I have to knock down one of these walls and extend the stall into the next one—but I’m going to watch you try that on.” Dropping the bags at my feet, I leaned back against the wall, arms crossed over my chest as I waited.

Sighing dramatically, she pulled off her shirt, revealing the gray bra she was already wearing. Reaching behind her, she unclasped it and let it fall at her feet before reaching for the new bra.

Seeing her bare from the waist up had me biting my fist to keep from groaning out loud. The freckle just under her left areola had my mouth watering, wanting to lick and taste it again. I loved that damn freckle.

Lyla turned her back to me as she pulled on the bra. “Fasten me, would you?”

I'd been fighting without myself not to touch her, but as soon as my fingers skimmed across the silky skin of her back while fastening it in place, I lost the battle. I dropped my hands to her waist, pulling her roughly back against me. She gasped excitedly as my rock-hard cock pulsed against her lower back, and the evil woman wiggled her hips into me.

Lowering my head, I kissed her neck, nipping at her flesh, and causing goose bumps to trail down her shoulders and arms.

"How does it feel?" I asked, looking at her in the mirror over her shoulder. "Do you like it?"

"It feels huge and hard. Fuck yeah, I like it."

Grinning, I kissed her temple. "I meant the bra, babe."

"Oh, it's fine. Do you like it?"

I looked down at her chest in the mirror. The bra pushed her tits up, but the cups only covered half of them, the straps crisscrossing over her cleavage. I liked the baby-pink color against her skin tone.

Keeping one hand on her hip to hold her against me, I lifted the other to skim across the top of her chest. “You’re so fucking beautiful, Lyla,” I breathed at her ear. “Tell me you’re mine, baby.”

“I’m yours,” she whispered, arching her neck so she could look back at me. “I always have been.”

“And you always will be,” I vowed, spinning her around to face me. My mouth crashed down on hers, my tongue thrusting deep to taste all of her. She wrapped her arms around my neck, and she climbed me until her legs were wrapped tightly around my waist and she was rocking against my erection.

“Fuck,” I growled when I lifted my head, mentally telling myself I really couldn’t fuck her in this tiny-ass changing room. “If you were wearing a dress, I’d already be inside you.”

“I’ll have to start wearing more of them, then,” she said before licking her kiss-swollen lips. “Better put me down before we do something that gets us arrested.”

“Don’t wanna,” I grumbled with a pout.

Lyla giggled, her hands stroking down my neck in a way that was meant to be soothing but only made me ache that much more. “Let me get dressed and pay for this, and after one more store, I promise we can go home."

Blowing out a heavy exhale, I untangled her legs from around me. "Fine. But I'm going to want cuddle time all evening."

"Whatever you want, my love."

I stole another kiss before she got dressed, and then I picked up all the bags and let her walk out before me.

It was almost another hour before we finally left, but she'd gotten Mia a birthday present she was sure her friend would love and was happily humming to herself as she walked beside me with her hand tucked into the crook of my elbow. I kept stealing glances at her, loving how much she was glowing. Happiness seemed to shine out of her, and it was addictive to look at.

"Why is that guy standing beside the SUV like that?" she asked, a frown wrinkling her brow.

I tensed and followed her gaze to where I'd parked the Suburban earlier. There was a guy who looked like he was in his midforties, dressed in jeans and a pullover, standing at the back of the SUV, his hands on his hips as he stared down at something on my vehicle. I didn't recognize the man, and as we got closer, I put myself between him and Lyla.

"Can I help you?" I asked, catching the man's attention.

He lifted his head. "This yours?" I nodded. "Looks like you're going to need a tow truck, buddy."

"What the fuck do you mean?" But as I rounded the corner of the SUV, I saw exactly what he meant.

I hadn't even noticed the vehicle leaning awkwardly at first, too focused on the stranger standing beside it. But both tires on that side had been slashed, the front had a screwdriver sticking out of it, the back, some weird-looking knife. The entire driver's side was scratched up, but what caught my attention the most were the words carved deeper into the door than the other scratches.

Whore!

Behind me, Lyla snorted. "She has a lot of balls calling me a whore."

I turned back to the stranger. "Did you see who did this?"

"Sorry, bud. I just got here." He pointed up at the poles with street lights and security cameras on them. "Maybe you will get lucky and they caught something. Good luck."

As he walked away, I glanced around, looking for any sign of Gwen or anyone else who might have done this. Not that I thought it was anyone other than my psycho ex.

Frustrated, I opened the back of the SUV and tossed in all the shopping bags. "Let's go," I told Lyla, taking her hand and keeping her close to me as we walked back into the mall. As we did, I called Judge.

"I'll be there in ten," he muttered, sounding frustrated. "Seriously, this bitch has got to go."

"Agreed, my friend."

In the security office, they showed me the camera feed from the moment I parked until we came out. Someone dressed in black leggings and a black hoodie with the hood pulled up over their head got out of an older-model sedan and casually walked up to my SUV. They were so short, the camera couldn't pick up what was happening on the other side of my massive vehicle, but it did show the Suburban starting to lean after the tires were shanked.

The whole thing took ten minutes, and during that time, several other cars drove by. But the culprit didn't seem to be in any hurry to complete the vandalism any more than if Lyla or I had shown up and caught her in the act.

It would have taken a lot of strength to get the screwdriver and knife into the tires, making me wonder just how Gwen was able to accomplish it with how weak I knew her to be. Unless she was so high she hurt herself thrusting the sharp objects into the thick rubber.

Wondering about that, I had the security guard rewind so I could look for any signs that she was injured. Sure enough, as the person in black made their way back to their own vehicle, they were holding their arm at an awkward angle.

"Bet she fucked up her broken wrist all over again," Lyla observed.

Clenching my jaw, I nodded, too pissed off to speak.

"She kept her face covered and averted the whole time so we can't prove it's Gwen, even though we know it's her," she said angrily.

“Meaning we have no proof that she broke the restraining order again.”

Gwen wasn’t totally stupid, but she was only digging herself deeper into a hole she would never be able to climb out of.

twenty

Lyla

After the craziness the day before had turned into, completely ruining the plans I'd had to stay in bed with Howler all evening, I was in desperate need of my best friend to vent to on Sunday.

Having gotten a text from Barrick the day before, I knew he and Mia were back together. Present in hand, I knocked on their door the next afternoon, feeling hopeful she was ready to forgive me too.

Braxton opened the door, his German Shepherd Sasha at his heel. "Hey," he greeted, stepping back to let me in. "Howler let you out of the house without him?"

I shrugged. "He and Judge were talking and I was bored with the conversation, so I stole the town car and the driver and came over." Turning, I waved at Tony, who was sitting in the driver's seat parked in the driveway.

He tilted his head in acknowledgment and backed out, knowing his boss wouldn't give him hell since I was with my cousins.

"Heard about the whole Gwen thing yesterday," Braxton commented as we walked into the living room. "Watch your back, cuz. That skank has lost her mind."

"Yeah," I muttered, sitting on the couch. Sasha sat down on the floor in front of me, putting her head on my knee. Without even thinking, I scratched her head, getting a happy whine from her in reward. "She's made everyone tense, and I'm getting tired of all this shit. I just want her to go away."

Laughter coming from the kitchen caught my attention. I recognized Mia's but the guy's didn't belong to Barrick. A moment later, my friend appeared, along with her date from Friday night.

I knew it was her friend Jordan, because Barrick had told me when I'd given him the keys to Howler's SUV Friday night as he was rushing to chase after her, but it still surprised the hell out of me that Barrick was okay with the guy being in his house. Especially when I suspected that Mia and Jordan hadn't always been just friends. The way

Jordan had looked at her the other night, I was fairly sure he'd seen her naked.

Jordan's eyes fell on me. "Well, hello there," he greeted, a smoldering look on his handsome face. "I'm Jordan Moreitti. What's your name, beautiful?"

Mia elbowed him in the ribs, hard. "Hands to yourself, dummy. This is Lyla, Barrick and Braxton's cousin."

His eyes danced with mirth. "So, you're a bodyguard too. Well, baby, you can guard my body any day of the week."

"Oh good gods, Jordan. Stop." She shoved him into a chair before flopping down on the couch beside me.

I quickly thrust the gift into her hands. "Please don't be mad at me anymore."

"Don't lie to me again," she said, pointing a finger at me. "I mean it."

"Technically, I didn't lie," I reminded her. "I just didn't tell you the whole truth."

Mia's green eyes narrowed on me warningly.

"Okay, okay. I swear on my brother's life, I will never lie or keep anything from you again." I crossed my heart then pointed at the bag. "Happy day before your birthday."

"You shouldn't have," she said, but she was already pulling the tissue paper out of the bag.

When she saw the Alex and Ani bracelet I'd created for her, she gasped softly. The charms had screamed Mia when I saw them. One was a pair of ballet slippers, the other simply read "inspire." Even in the short time she'd been Josie's dance teacher, I'd seen just how gifted Mia truly was. All of her students loved and looked up to her, and I was glad she was the one who was getting Josie to fall in love with dancing.

Sliding the bracelet onto her wrist, she threw her arms around me, sniffling suspiciously. "Thank you so much. I love it."

I hugged her back tightly, glad she wasn't pissed at me anymore. "Don't cry. Barrick and Braxton will kill me if I make you cry."

"Fuck yeah, I will," my older cousin growled as he walked into the living room from the back of the house. He took one look at us, saw the tears in Mia's eyes, and pointed at the door. "Out, Lyla. If you're going to make her cry, you're not welcome here."

"Wait!" Mia rushed to correct him. "Happy tears, Beast." She showed him her wrist with the bracelet. "Look at what she gave me for my birthday. Isn't it pretty?"

"Beautiful," he agreed, bending to kiss her forehead. When he lifted his head, his eyes were a little calmer. "I guess you can stay, then."

"Way to shit on everyone else's present, Lyla," Braxton grumbled.

I lifted my brows at him. "What did you give her?"

"I'm not saying. Haven't given it to her yet," he said with a shrug. "Her birthday is tomorrow."

"What about you?" I asked Jordan, who was watching us all like we were an entertaining sitcom. "What did you give the birthday girl?"

"Mia isn't all that into presents. So, I flew out to spend the weekend with her. Not that we spent a lot of time together." He shot her a mock glare.

"I said I was sorry," she said sheepishly.

"I don't see a single ounce of remorse in those pretty green eyes for ditching me yesterday," he teased.

"What time is your flight again?" Barrick asked, pulling the other guy's attention to him.

"Four. So I have to get on the road soon since I have to turn in my rental."

"Are you sure you can't stay one more night?" Mia asked hopefully. "Please?"

"I wish I could, love," he told her regretfully. "But I promise I'll see you again before I go to Italy."

It wasn't long before he was saying goodbye. Mia seemed upset, but Barrick led her to their room to cheer her up. I took that as my cue to go.

"See you tomorrow," I told Braxton as he walked me out to the waiting cab I'd called because Tony hadn't answered when I'd tried to call him. No doubt I'd catch hell for not waiting on my brother's driver, but I really just wanted to go home.

"Watch your back, Lyla." Opening the rear door for me, he gave me a quick hug before stepping back. "If you need anything, call me."

"Yeah. Love ya, Brax."

"Love you too, Ly."

Walking into the house a little while later, I could hear Judge and Howler still talking in the kitchen, but there was no sign of Josie. Missing her, I texted Cherie to see when she was bringing Josie home or if we needed to pick her up.

I didn't get an immediate reply, and I debated just going over and picking her up right then.

"…can't fucking make me choose, Judge. Stop being a dick, and just deal with it."

I stiffened when I heard what Howler was saying. Stopping midstep, I paused, waiting to listen as my heart started pounding out of control, practically holding my breath as I strained to hear.

"Just because you're unhappy right now with this Ellianna shit doesn't mean you get to go throwing your weight around and fucking up everyone else's happiness."

"This isn't about me or Ellianna," Judge told him in a hard voice. "This is about Lyla and her safety. Her happiness. When was the last time you even had a long-term relationship? Gwen? And how well did that end, Howler?"

"Because it's always been Lyla for me. I love her, man. And I'm not giving her up."

I closed my eyes, finally able to take a deep enough breath once again.

"Not even if I say you're banned from the Underground? No more fights. No more—"

"Not even then, asshole. Take it away. Ban me. Stop being my friend. I don't fucking care. I was stupid all these years, picking you and everything else over her. That's over now. I won't let you or anyone else stand in my way."

Tears blurred my vision, and I had to cover my mouth with both hands to keep from sobbing.

He really is choosing me.

twenty-one

Howler

The savage look on Judge's face slowly morphed into a grin.

"About damn time you smartened up," my best friend said with a smile as he slapped me on the back.

"What the fuck, man?" I demanded, pushing him away.

"Relax. I'm not actually making you choose, dumbass. Just making sure you pulled your head out of your ass and got your priorities straight." He picked up his beer and drained it before dropping it in the recycling. "When's Lyla supposed to be ho…me? Fuck."

I turned at his muttered curse to find Lyla standing in the kitchen doorway, hands on her hips as she glared from me to her brother.

"Now, Lyla, just listen," Judge began, his hands raised defensively.

"No, you listen, Zachary Bennet. If you ever—and I mean fucking ever—pull this shit again, I will cut you out of my life so fast you'll get whiplash." She pointed at the door. "Now, get the hell out. I want you out of my face for the foreseeable future."

"Right, okay." He nodded nervously. "I'm sorry, Lyla. Don't be mad. I was only—"

"I don't want to hear it," she snapped at him. "Just go."

I stood there, holding my breath as Judge shot me an apologetic grimace and made a run for it. Lyla didn't move until the door slammed in the distance. When it did, she turned to face me, and I nearly dropped to my knees in front of her when I saw the tears in her eyes.

"Baby—"

"You picked me," she whispered.

"Of course, I picked you. Did you think I wouldn't?" Before she could answer, I lifted my hands. "Don't answer that. I think your answer will make me want to kick my own ass." Moving forward, I was finally able to breathe when I wrapped my arms around her. "I love you so damn much, Lyla. I'm so sorry it's taken so long for me to put you first, but I swear on everything that is holy, I'll never make that mistake again."

Her smile was trembling when she looked up at me. "I believe you."

I wanted to take her upstairs, but Josie was likely to come home at any time. Instead, I made do with a kiss that had her falling weakly against me, clinging to my shoulders until we heard the front door opening minutes later.

I lifted my head as I heard little feet running through the house. "Daddy! Grandma and I made cupcakes. Do you want one?"

I stepped back from Lyla to find Josie standing beside us with a container of cupcakes. Bending, I lifted her up and placed her on the counter before unboxing the dessert.

"Oh my goodness, Jo. These look so yummy," Lyla told her as she pulled one from the container and bit into it. "Yup. Best cupcakes I've ever tasted."

Beaming, Josie started telling us about how hard she'd worked on decorating the treats as my mom walked in.

The next day, Lyla went to work with me again, but she left early to get ready for her night out. She was meeting Mia Armstrong's parents and having dinner to celebrate Mia's birthday. When Josie and I got home, the house felt empty without her.

"Is Lyla coming home tonight?" Josie asked hopefully as we ate the pizza I'd picked up on the way home.

"Yeah, Jo. She's just having dinner with Miss Mia," I assured her.

"Oh yeah." But not thirty minutes later, as I helped her get ready for bed, she sighed heavily. "I wish Lyla was home already."

"Me too, sunshine. Me too." But Lyla had told me she wouldn't be back until at least after ten, and that was still a while away. I was glad she'd made up with her friend and they were spending time together, but I missed her. Now that I knew what it was like to have Lyla beside me twenty-four seven, I hated being without her for even a few hours.

"Daddy—" She broke off hesitantly, but I could tell she wanted to ask me something.

"What's wrong, Josie?" I urged, keeping my tone soft.

"I want Lyla to live with us forever," she finally blurted out, pink filling her cheeks. "Can't you marry her and she can stay with us and she can be my new mommy?"

I stopped with my hand lifted to brush her hair. Tossing the brush on the bathroom vanity, I turned her to face me. "Is that what you really want, Jo? You want me to marry Lyla?"

She was nodding adamantly before I'd even finished the first question. "Please, Daddy. Please. We love Lyla, right? And she loves us. She takes good care of us, and I like having a mommy who doesn't hit me and gives me cuddles."

My heart broke for my little girl at the thought of her biological mother treating her like shit. I should have done something a hell of a lot sooner, should have known something wasn't right with them. I was never going to forgive myself for not realizing it earlier.

"You're right, baby girl. And I am going to ask Lyla to marry me, but let's not tell her yet. Okay?"

"Like a secret?" she whispered.

I grinned. "Yeah. A secret. One only you and I know about. Not even Uncle Judge will know we want to marry Lyla and make her ours."

She gave me a sly little grin and, like always, I was startled by how much my beautiful daughter looked like me. “Okay, Daddy. But can you marry Lyla soon? I really, really, really want to call her mommy.”

“Very, very soon, kiddo,” I promised.

twenty-two

Lyla

I was running late to pick up Josie. She normally didn't go to school on Tuesdays, but we were slowly easing her into going the full five days. This was her first week attending four days instead of the usual three. I'd gotten distracted with a new project Howler was thinking of doing, so when I realized what time it was, I started scrambling to get out the door.

"Hey, hey," Howler called as he came out of his office. His sleeves were rolled up to his elbows, and the top buttons of his shirt were undone, giving me a tantalizing view of his sexy chest. "Slow down, baby. They aren't going to hold Josie for ransom just because you're a few minutes late."

Grabbing me by the hips, he pulled me in for a slow, deep kiss. When he lifted his head, I was able to breathe a little deeper, and I melted against him. Smirking down at me, he kissed the tip of my nose. "You're amazing, you know that?"

I blinked up at him, surprised by his comment. "How so?"

"How you love Josie so much, you freak out that you're a little behind picking her up. How you take such good care of her—and me." He kissed his way down my neck, not even caring that other staff in the office could see us. That his mother could see us. "I don't know how I got so lucky that you love me and my daughter so damn much, but I'm thankful, Lyla."

"Stop," I whispered fiercely, fighting tears. "You're going to make me cry."

"Sorry, babe." Kissing me again, he gave my ass a firm squeeze then stepped back. "Go. I'll see you tonight. Hopefully I won't be too much longer, and I can pick you and Josie up after her dance class."

"Take your time. I got this." Blowing him a kiss, I rushed out the door.

Tony was already waiting for me in the parking lot, and no sooner was I in the back seat than he was pulling out into traffic to go get Josie. Of all the security my brother had working for him, Tony was on the newer side, but he drove me almost every time I needed it. We only ever talked long enough for me to tell him where I was going, and I got the feeling he would rather do anything but drive me around like some glorified chauffeur. But my brother paid him well, so he never voiced any complaints that I knew of.

He pulled up in front of the preschool, and I didn't wait for him to open my door before I was getting out and sprinting into the building. Thankfully, Josie wasn't even close to being the last student for pickup, and she didn't seem upset that I was later than usual.

Bouncing over to me, she threw her arms around both my legs. "I drew Miss Mia a birthday card during art time today," she announced, showing me the folded piece of pink construction paper. "Do you think she will like it?"

I opened it to find a stick figure ballet dancer with red hair and a sloppily written "Happy Birthday! Love, Josie" across the bottom. It was the most precious birthday card I'd ever seen.

"I think she's going to love it, Jo," I assured her.

Her teacher came over to join us, bringing Josie's backpack. "We had a great day today, Miss Bennet," the woman informed me.

"Awesome. Thanks. Sorry I was late."

She waved off my apology with a laugh. "Five minutes is nothing, trust me."

Once Josie had her jacket on, I took her hand and we left. We got home with just enough time for her to have a quick snack and change for dance class before we had to leave again.

As we climbed into the back of the town car once more, I told Tony we were going to the dance school, and he nodded. But when he backed out of the driveway, he didn't turn in the direction we needed to go.

"Are we going to Daddy's work before class?" Josie asked casually as she glanced out the side window from her booster seat.

"Tony," I called up to him. "This isn't the way to Cora's."

His hands tightened around the wheel, and from where I was sitting, I saw a muscle tick in his jaw, but he didn't answer.

"Tony, what are you doing?" I demanded, already pulling my phone from my purse to call Judge and bitch about the driver.

The car slammed to a stop so suddenly, both Josie and I jerked forward against the restraints of our seat belts, and Josie squealed in fright. Before I could even right myself or reach for her, Tony grabbed my phone out of my hand and tossed it out the window.

On instinct, I grasped Josie's hand and reached for the door handle while we were still stopped, but the handle moved without opening. I barely had time to realize the child safety locks were engaged—which they hadn't been when we'd gotten home earlier—before Tony was stomping on the gas. The tires burned rubber as he sped in the direction he'd been heading only moments before.

"Lyla, what's happening?" Josie asked tearfully, fear shining out of her blue eyes like a beacon.

"I don't know, baby girl," I whispered, moving closer to her, shielding her from Tony and any other danger that might come our way. "But I won't let anything happen to you. I promise."

Howler

I was so engrossed in the plans I was working on that needed to be done before I could go home, that when my phone rang, I almost let it go to voice mail. But at the last second, I picked up, barely noticing it was Barrick calling.

"What's up, man?"

"Hey, Mia is worried about Josie. Is she sick?"

I dropped my pencil, remembering the last time I'd gotten a call from one of Lyla's cousins saying Mia was worried about my daughter. "Not that I know of. Why? Is she acting weird?"

"I wouldn't know. Josie didn't show up for class."

My eyes dropped to the clock on my desk, and I cursed. It was already twenty minutes after the normal time for her class to start. "Lyla was supposed to drop her off. Let me call her, and I'll call you back."

"Sure. She didn't answer when I tried to call her before you, but maybe she was just busy."

"Lyla isn't answering her phone?" My gut clenched with trepidation. "I'll call you back," I told him distractedly. I disconnected and started calling Lyla's number. But it went straight to voice mail without even ringing once.

Muttering a curse, I called Judge. "Something's wrong," I told him as soon as he said hello. "Josie didn't show up for dance, and Lyla isn't answering her phone."

"Maybe Josie just didn't feel like going tonight," he suggested. "Didn't you say she was going to school an extra day this week? She's probably just tired, brother."

"No," I snapped. "Not Josie. She would want to go to dance even if she were puking her guts out. She loves that class and her teacher. Call your driver. Find out what's going on."

"Yeah, okay. I'm on it, man. Give me a second, and I'll call you back."

I jerked to my feet and was already at my SUV before my phone rang again. "Well?" I demanded as I jumped into the driver's seat and started the vehicle.

"He's not fucking answering. I turned on the LoJack GPS on the car, and you're going to blow a gasket when I tell you where the car is."

"Just say it," I roared, past the point of no return without even knowing what the hell was going on. All I wanted to know was where my girls were and how long it would take me to get to them.

"There's one particular drug den Gwen has been frequenting lately, from what I could tell. The car is parked at that address." Judge's voice was laced with ice and steel, but I didn't have time to ask what the hell else was wrong. I needed to get to Lyla and Josie.

"Where?" I snapped, and he read off the address. I knew roughly where that was and didn't take the time to punch it into the GPS.

Without another word to my friend, I hung up and called Barrick back.

"Goddamn it!" Lyla's cousin exploded. "I fucking told Judge not to hire outside people. All he had to do was ask me, and I could have gotten him an entire detail that he could trust."

"You saying I can't trust Tony?"

"I'm saying, unless they come from Seller, you can't trust anyone. Give me the address. I'm on my way now."

"Barrick…" I hesitated, knowing he would be the only person who could really answer me. "Lyla… Will she be okay?"

"Howler, man, you gotta trust her right now. She's good at her job. You and Judge never wanted to believe that, but she is. My stepdad never would have given me the okay to hire her if she weren't one of the best."

His assurance did nothing to help ease any of my fear for her or Josie. Gwen had a gun. I pressed my foot harder on the gas, praying I got to them in time.

twenty-three

Lyla

It was dark outside when the car came to a stop. There were no streetlights and only a few lights on in some of the houses we passed, making it hard to tell where we were, but I knew this part of town was not a place I would ever willingly take Josie.

The house Tony stopped in front of had a single light on in what I assumed was the living room. Even with the poor lighting, I could tell there were broken windows, and the porch looked like a stiff wind would send the thing crashing down.

Tony got out and opened Josie's door, but when he reached in for her, it was to find her already on the other side of me, my body protecting her from him.

He gave me a grin that made me want to scratch up his face. "We can do this the easy way or the hard way, Lyla."

I shot him a scathing look. "You touch her, and I promise you won't live to breathe another day."

He shrugged. "I won't touch her. You can even carry the brat, for all I care." He pulled something from behind him, and Josie screamed, her tiny fingers fisting in the material of my jacket when she saw the barrel of the gun he must have taken from a holster. "But if you don't get out now, there won't be anything but a lifeless body for you to carry. Feel me?"

I didn't think he had the balls to pull the trigger on anyone, but I wasn't about to test that theory. "Okay, okay," I told him, keeping my voice calm so I didn't scare Josie more than she already was. "Just back up, and we will get out."

He moved two steps back but no more. I took what I was given and climbed out, pulling Josie by the hand along behind me until my feet were on the ground. Turning my back on Tony went against everything I'd ever been taught and my instincts were screaming to keep my eyes on him every second, but I needed to hold on to Josie.

Bending, I lifted her into my arms. Her limbs wrapped around me so tightly, it was hard to breathe for just a moment. I kissed her cheek and told her everything was going to be all right, and she eased up her hold enough for me to take in a deep breath.

As we walked toward the house, her little body trembled against me, and I tried to soothe her as much as I could.

"My mommy's in there," she whispered against my chest where she had her face buried.

"How do you know, Jo?" I asked quietly.

"Because she took me here before."

"Of course she did," I muttered, even more pissed at the thought of Gwen bringing my baby to this disgusting place. I could smell the dry rot in the wood of the rattrap of a porch, but something more stomach-turning was coming from the broken windows. It smelled like sour urine and raw sewage, making me wonder if there was actual plumbing in there or if people just popped a squat anywhere and used the bathroom wherever they chose.

The stairs protested loudly as I walked up them to the porch, just as the front door opened and Gwen stepped out of the weak lighting glowing behind her. I barely saw the outline of the gun in her hands as she staggered forward.

Thinking she meant to take Josie from me, I tightened my hold on her and sidestepped Gwen when she moved in our direction. Tony pushed me forward, and I stumbled several steps before I was able to right myself, causing Josie to scream and start sobbing.

"Shh, shh," I hushed her. "It's okay. I won't let anything happen to you, sweetheart."

"I don't want them to hurt you," she whispered so low I almost didn't hear her. "Mommy hates you."

I was no fan of hers either, but I kept that to myself as I continued to rub Josie's back while taking in the layout of the house I'd just been pushed into. The smell was a hundred times worse inside than what was drifting out the broken windows. I wanted to gag, but I fought against it hard. Josie would probably vomit if I did, and who knew what either Gwen or Tony would do if that happened.

It was a single-story house with an open layout. From where I was standing in the living room, I could see the kitchen at the back of the house, and two doors were open, one of which was a bathroom, where the smell of excrement was the worst, and the other was a bedroom. I didn't want to know what kind of bodily fluids were flowing around in there any more than I wanted an up close and personal tour of the bathroom.

I counted the doors, the possible exits, and the windows, mapping out in my head what I could see of the place and trying to decide the best escape plan while still carrying the extra weight of a little girl. Tony pushed me again, this time toward the couch that looked like it was infested with a lot worse than just bedbugs, and I was thankful I'd put Josie's hair up in a bun before we left the house. Mine, however, was still hanging around my shoulders, and I dreaded sitting down but I did before Tony could start pushing me again.

"They're here. Now what?" Tony demanded of Gwen, who was just standing beside him, glaring at me with dilated, bloodshot eyes.

Fuck, of course she was high. No doubt she stayed that way these days now that she didn't have the responsibility of tending to a child. She'd even been high the night I'd kicked her skanky ass.

I glanced at her casted wrist. Her arms were covered with a long-sleeved shirt, but I could see the outline of the cast under it. She was holding her arm awkwardly, though, and I remembered the way she'd cradled it on the security video from the mall after she'd slashed Howler's tires.

I was sure she'd broken it again, and I kept that in mind as I went back to mapping our escape.

"Now, we wait. Howler will come for them. And then I'll take care of them all," Gwen told him with a laugh before sniffing loudly.

My hands tightened around Josie without realizing, and she whined her protest because I was squeezing her too hard.

Gwen couldn't hurt Howler. I wouldn't let her hurt anyone I loved, but especially not Josie and Howler.

My mind started working furiously, trying to come up with something—fucking anything—that would get us out of this hellhole before Howler showed up and got himself killed trying to save us.

"You're a twisted bitch, Gwen," Tony told her, but there was a wicked grin on his face. "Wanting to off these two in front of Howler. You gonna kill him after?"

"Nope," Gwen answered, amusement lacing her raspy voice. "Let the fucker live, knowing I took everything he loves away from him. It's what he deserves for not loving me."

Ah hell. She'd really lost her mind if she thought she could do that. But I didn't tell her that. I kept my mouth shut, not giving either of them a reason to turn their attention on either Josie or me.

Instead, I kept glancing at the bathroom. I noticed a window open in there, but it was higher up. Josie would be able to fit through it, but she wouldn't be able to climb up to it without help.

The bedroom was too dark to be able to see if the window was open in there or not, making it hard for me to decide where to send Josie if things got crazy before I could get her out myself.

"Josie." I had my lips right up against her ear, pretending to kiss her and soothe her as I rocked her little body. "If you can hear me, nod, baby girl." She nodded her head ever so slightly. "In a moment, I'm going to set you on your feet. When I do, I want you to go into the bedroom and shut the door. Lock it if you can. Then I want you to try the window. If it's open, climb out and run. If it's not, climb under the bed."

“But…” she whispered, but I shushed her.

“I’ll be right behind you as quickly as I can. Just run, Jo. You understand?” Again, I got a nod, but I could feel her tears soaking my shirt.

Tony was the bigger threat of the two, so I waited until he started to relax his guard and turned his back to us. When he did, I moved fast, putting Josie on her feet while Gwen wasn’t paying attention and whispered for her to run. I jumped up and ran up behind Tony as quietly as I could.

But before I could reach him, he turned, his gun pointed right at my chest. Behind me, I heard the bedroom door shut, and the click of the lock made it easier to do what I had to do.

His finger moved to the trigger just as I lifted my hand to knock the gun out of his hold. He wasn’t expecting the power I put behind the hit, and he lost control of the weapon even as he was pulling the trigger.

I felt the bullet burn across my skin as it nicked my shoulder through my jacket, but I didn’t let myself think about it as I kicked him in the balls then the stomach and sent him crashing down to his knees. Using my knee, I busted his nose, then dropped my elbow down on the back of his head.

He fell flat on the dirty floor, groaning.

Praying Josie was able to get out the bedroom window, I turned just as Gwen lifted her own gun and pointed it right at my heart. Her hands shook, making the gun waver, and I walked toward her, pretending like I wasn't scared of her.

"You never should have fucked with me, Gwen," I told her as I got closer. Face devoid of color, she backed up farther and farther until the wall stopped her. "You never should have messed with what was mine. And you never, fucking never, should have touched Josie."

One hand wrapped around the barrel of her gun, I snatched it from her hands before easily turning it on her. My hand was steady as I pointed it in her face, pressing the metal flush against the skin between her eyes. "Your daughter is mine now, and I'll treasure her for the rest of my life, like you should have but were too selfish. You are nothing but trash, you junkie whore. I'll personally make sure you never come near her again."

"P-please," Gwen stuttered, her wild eyes begging me not to hurt her. "Don't kill me. Josie… Sh-she won't ever forgive you if you kill me."

"I'm not going to kill you, bitch," I promised her. "Just make you wish you were dead."

She furrowed her brows, trying to figure out what I could possibly mean by that, even as I drew back and punched her in the face so hard, her eyes rolled back in her head and she dropped at my feet.

Behind me, I heard Tony moving, and I turned when I heard his heavy footsteps. The moment he started toward me, an angry snarl on his face, I had the gun lifted and, out of instinct, pulled the trigger.

The impact of the bullet to his left shoulder had him jerking backward, blood squirting from the hole I'd just put in him, but it didn't stop him. If anything, it only pissed him off more, and his speed increased.

I shot him again, this time dead center in the chest, and I knew before he even fell to his knees that I'd just taken his life.

twenty-four

Howler

My tires screamed in protest when I came to a sudden stop right beside the town car. I jumped out of the SUV and started running toward the house.

"Daddy!"

Josie's scream had me stopping in my tracks as my daughter came running from around the side of the house. The only light was coming from the living room, but I could still see the tears running down her face as she flung herself at me.

I scooped her up, holding her trembling little body against me and thanking God she was alive. "Daddy," Josie sobbed. "Lyla is in there."

"It's okay, Jo. I'll get her." I rushed back to the vehicle and put her in the back seat. "Stay here. Uncle Judge and Uncle Barrick are on their way."

"Daddy, I'm scared," she cried. "Mommy is going to hurt Lyla."

"No, she won't, baby girl. I promise." I tried to give her a reassuring smile, but just as I stepped back to close the door, I heard a gun going off.

Josie screamed, and I suddenly felt like I couldn't breathe. I locked the door as I shut it and took off running. Before I could get to the steps, the sound of another shot echoed through the air, and I started shouting Lyla's name.

"Lyla!" I roared as I kicked open the front door and ran inside.

My eyes found her first. She was standing in the middle of the living room, a gun still extended and pointed at the man who was now lying lifeless on the floor only feet away from her. Blood was gushing out of Tony, flooding the cheat carpet around him.

I quickly looked around, saw Gwen lying on the floor, and didn't even care if she was dead or not. Making sure there were no other threats to my girl, I rushed her. She turned at the sound of my footsteps, and the gun turned with her.

Seeing it was me, she dropped the weapon at her feet and started to crumple. "Howler," she sobbed. "I had to. I-I…I had to."

I folded my arms around her, pulling her against me, and I began to tremble just as badly as Josie had been when I found her. "It's okay, baby. I know. It's not your fault." I kissed her temple, her cheek, and then her lips, too thankful she was alive to fight back the tears of relief starting to fall. "I've got you, Lyla."

Her arms went around me, and she buried her face in my chest. "I had to," she whispered brokenly.

Behind me, I heard Barrick come in. "Told you she had this," he muttered as he took stock of the room. He walked over to Gwen and crouched down to feel for a pulse. "She's alive."

"I-I only knocked her out," Lyla told him shakily. "I didn't mean to kill T-Tony."

"Of course not, sweetheart," her cousin told her soothingly as he walked over to embrace her. "It was self-defense."

"Lyla!" Judge shouted as he stormed into the house. His face was white as a ghost as he rushed over and pulled her into his arms. "Are you okay?" He ran his hands over her, and she whimpered in pain when he touched her right shoulder.

That was when I saw the hole in her black jacket. I pulled her away from Judge and started taking off her jacket. She cried out as I jarred her arm, but I was too worried about the blood.

"It's only a graze." She tried to play it off. "I'm fine."

"Get her to the hospital," Judge commanded. "Barrick and I will deal with this shit. The cops are already on their way."

I picked her up and ran from the house. Josie was standing up in the back, her face pressed to the window as she watched me coming. I clicked the fob to unlock the door before I reached her, and I placed Lyla in the back seat with my daughter before jumping behind the wheel. I left tread marks on the asphalt as I took off for the nearest hospital.

"Lyla, are you okay?" Josie was asking as I took a hard right.

"I'm fine, baby girl," Lyla assured her. "How about you? Nothing hurts?"

"I'm just scared for you," the little girl told her, crying again. "Lyla, you're bleeding!"

"Nothing a stitch or two won't fix, love bug. Come here and give me cuddles."

I chanced a glance in the rearview mirror to see Josie curled up in Lyla's arms. Even though she was hurt, Lyla was calming my kid. From the moment Josie was born, Lyla had loved her.

There was a hospital only a few miles away, and I pulled up in front of the ER. Getting out, I carried Lyla inside and yelled for them to help me.

"Howler, I'm fine. Really."

Ignoring her, I looked around frantically. I wasn't going to take Lyla's word on this. She was probably just trying to soothe me, when I was terrified I was going to lose her at any second.

The place wasn't very busy, and a nurse came out with a wheelchair, asking what had happened as I placed Lyla in the chair.

"She's been shot," I told the woman and picked up Josie, who had run in with us, holding my hand.

The nurse glanced at Lyla's arm and sighed. "She'll live, sir. I promise." Smiling down at Lyla, she started pushing her into the back to an exam room. "Let's get you fixed up, hon. Doc, can you come stitch this poor girl up before her man has a stroke?"

It took less than an hour for them to do an X-ray, just to be sure that nothing was broken, and then stitch her up. They gave her some antibiotics to keep her from getting an infection and a prescription for pain medication before they released her.

We were on our way out the door when Judge and Barrick pulled up in front of the hospital. Judge came over to us, his face set in stone as his eyes scanned over his sister from head to toe.

"How are you feeling?"

She gave him a grim smile, her arm in a sling against her chest to keep it immobile while it healed. "I'm good. I swear. You and Howler need to relax. It was just a scratch."

I kissed the top of her head and tucked her closer. "Everything taken care of?"

"Yeah. They are writing it off as self-defense, but the cops will be at your house around lunchtime tomorrow to get Lyla's statement. I'll come over and make sure they don't overtire her." He hugged her, but I didn't move back so he could get more than one arm around her. Now that I was sure she was okay, I wasn't about to release her to allow something else to happen to her. "Gwen is in custody, and I've already called the DA to make sure they deny her bail."

Barrick hugged her next, then smiled at Josie. "Miss Mia says she hopes you're okay, Josie. And that you will be in class next week."

"She'll be there. Won't you, brave girl?" Lyla said, giving her a warm smile.

Josie nodded. "I made her a card for her birthday, but I think I lost it."

"We'll make her another one," Lyla promised her then fought back a yawn. "But tomorrow. I can't seem to keep my eyes open."

Barrick kissed her cheek. "Call Mia tomorrow, or she's going to freak out and come over. Which means Braxton and I will descend on you, little cuz."

"Is Brax with Mia now?" she asked.

"Yeah, him and her folks. They're staying a few days and making sure everything is settled for Mia's cousin to move in with us after Christmas." Barrick kissed Josie on top of her head then stepped back. "Call me if you need me, guys." His gaze landed on Judge. "And tomorrow, we are getting you a whole new security detail. We clear, asshat?"

“Yeah, whatever,” Judge grumbled.

“I’m taking my girls home,” I told Judge when it was just him and us standing there. “Lyla needs some rest, and I know Josie is hungry.”

“Yeah, okay. Just be careful.” He kissed both Lyla and Josie, and then he shook my hand. “I’ll talk to you tomorrow.” He turned to go then stopped and looked back at his sister. “I love you, Lyla.”

“Love you, Judge,” she told him sleepily.

On the drive home, both Lyla and Josie fell asleep, and once we were in the driveway, I just sat there for a long while, watching them. This was one of the worst nights of my life, but it could have been so much more tragic. I could have lost one or both of them, and I couldn’t live without either of them.

Scrubbing my hands over my face, I let the stress of the past few hours press down on me. I needed to get both of them inside and into bed, probably make us all something to eat, but I couldn’t bring my muscles to cooperate.

“Howler?” Lyla’s soft voice reached out for me in the darkened vehicle.

I dropped my hands and leaned toward her. "What's wrong, babe?"

"I really am okay," she said as she lifted her left hand and cupped the side of my face. "You don't have to worry about me now."

I turned my head so I could kiss her palm. "I'm always worried about you when you're not right beside me. Nothing will ever change that."

"I'm so sorry about putting Josie in danger," she whispered suddenly, her chin trembling. "If anything had happened to her—"

"You protected her, and for that, I will always be thankful. You're everything a mother should be, Lyla. And that is exactly what you are to Josie. She wants you to be, you know. She asked me the other day…"

Her eyes widened. "What did she ask?"

"If I would marry you so she could start calling you 'Mommy,'" I told her honestly.

"Daddy!" Josie surprised me by yelling. "It was supposed to be our secret."

I grinned at her over my shoulder as she unfastened her seat belt and stood up between us. "Sorry, Jo. Tonight has been so crazy that I just couldn't help myself."

"Wait," Lyla protested, touching her head dazedly. "These pain pills are making me loopy. What are you two talking about?"

Leaning forward, I kissed her lips but quickly pulled back. "Nothing, babe. We're not talking about anything. At least, not tonight. Sit tight, and I'll get you into the house."

"Ugh," she muttered. "You're so annoying sometimes."

epilogue

Lyla

The cops came and went the next day after taking a quick statement from me. My brother, on the other hand, lingered and tried to baby me all afternoon.

I let him do what he wanted, even though he was more irritating than helpful. He was just so adorable when he was trying to be sweet and I didn't get that side of him all that often, so I soaked it up for a little while until I couldn't take it any longer and kicked him out of the house.

"Is he finally gone?" Howler asked as he came out of his office where he'd been working since the cops left earlier. He'd called his mom and told her he wouldn't be at work that morning, then had to explain everything else that happened the day before because Cherie wasn't one to take a simple excuse. Especially from her son who worked every day even when he was sick.

He wrapped his arms around my waist as I nodded. “I told him to go home and not come back for a few days. He was getting on my last nerve.”

“He just loves you,” Howler defended. “I think you getting shot last night scared him almost as much as it did me.”

“Yeah,” I muttered, trying not to think about the events of the night before. Of Tony’s lifeless eyes staring at nothing. I’d taken a man’s life, and I didn’t know how to accept that.

“Hey,” he murmured, cupping my neck and using his thumb to tilt my head back so I had to look up at him. “It was you or him, and you made the right decision, baby. If something had happened to you, I would have lost my mind.”

Tears filled my eyes, but I nodded. “I know. I just… This is hard for me, Howler. I don’t know how to accept the fact that I ended someone’s life.”

“I’m so sorry, baby. Do you… I don’t know. Maybe want to talk to someone about this? Like a therapist or something?”

The way he hesitated, as if he didn’t know how to help me but was struggling to find any solution, warmed my heart, and I melted into him a little more. "Maybe. But not today. Right now, I just need to be here with you and Jo."

His smile melted more than my heart, and he bent to brush his lips over the tip of my nose. "I think I can arrange that. How about I make some popcorn, and we can watch a movie together until dinner?"

"I like that idea."

"Good. You go get our girl, and I'll fix the popcorn." With one more kiss, he turned me in his arms and urged me toward the stairs. "Tell Josie she can pick the movie."

Upstairs, I found Josie lying on the floor, all her art supplies laid out before her as she colored on a piece of folded construction paper. Smiling down at the sight of her so lost in concentration, I sat on the floor across from her.

"Is that the birthday card for Miss Mia?"

Josie shook her head as she continued writing something across the bottom of the card she was making. "No. I already made her a birthday card. It's just like the one I lost yesterday."

I picked up the folded construction paper. This one was purple, but when I opened it, there was the same stick-figured redhead in ballet slippers with

"Happy Birthday! Love, Josie" written in Josie's sloppy handwriting.

"Very pretty," I told her and replaced the card on the floor.

"There!" she exclaimed softly to herself as she closed the new card and stood up.

Bending, she picked up the card and handed it to me. On the front, it read "To Lyla. From Josie," and there were two stick figures underneath it. A little girl with blond hair and a taller female with dark hair like mine.

Seeing the two of us together like that made something tighten in my heart, and I opened the card with fingers that trembled.

On one side of the card, there was a rainbow and flowers and the two of us drawn again, still holding hands. But it was what was on the other side of the card that had tears filling my eyes until I couldn't even see the words anymore.

"Will you be my mommy?" was written in her messy, adorable handwriting, and I'd never seen more beautiful words in my life.

Dropping the card, I reached for her and pulled her down into my lap so I could bury my nose in her sweet-smelling hair. "Yes, Jo," I whispered in a voice choked with a million different emotions. "I would love to be your mommy."

"Really?" she yelled excitedly.

"Really," I laughed, my voice cracking.

"I'm so, so, so happy!" she cried, hugging me even as she bounced up and down on my lap. "Come on. Let's tell Daddy. I bet he will be happy too."

She pulled on my hand, and I got to my feet. My tears were still flowing, but I held her hand in one of my own while clutching the card she'd made for me in the other.

Downstairs, I could smell the popcorn he must have made, but when we got to the kitchen, there was no sign of Howler. Frowning, I looked around, wondering how I'd missed passing such a huge man along the way, but he wasn't anywhere.

"Come on, Lyla… I mean Mommy!" Josie tugged me to the French doors, and I opened them, surprised they were unlocked. Howler hadn't unlocked that door since Gwen had gotten in that first time.

It was a warmer than usual day outside, and we were both in long sleeves so I didn't make her go back in for a jacket. Instead, I let her pull me out to her play area.

But as we rounded the side of it, I nearly stumbled. There were white and red flower petals surrounding Howler in the shape of a giant heart as he knelt on the ground with a ring box already open in his hands. The little box looked so tiny in his massive palm, but the pear-shaped diamond nestled within it sparkled.

"Daddy, Lyla said yes," Josie told her father happily, bouncing around again. "She wants to be my mommy!"

He gave her a smile that looked nervous to me, but I wasn't sure because my tears were blinding me all over again. As I walked closer, he cleared his throat. "Lyla, yesterday was the worst day of my life. So easily, I could have lost you and Josie, and I'm so thankful I didn't. But today, I want to erase the nightmare and create happy memories I hope you will remember for the rest of your life." He swallowed hard and inhaled deeply. "Baby, I love you, and I'm tired of wasting time. This might seem sudden to you, but I've ached to ask you this for years. Please, will you marry me?"

"Howler," I breathed, shaking my head as tears fell down my face. "I love you so much."

"Is that…a yes?" he asked hesitantly.

Laughing, I threw myself against him, sending us both to the ground. "Yes," I sobbed. "Of course, yes."

My tears fell onto his face, but his soon joined them. I kissed him, and the memories of the day before, of Tony and Gwen and everything else but the happiness he and Josie had given me, faded for the moment.

Josie jumped onto my back, wanting to be a part of the excitement, and Howler wrapped his arms around her too. "You two are the most precious things in my world. I'm never letting either of you go again."

Coming Soon From Terri Anne Browning

Needing Nevaeh

Book 2 of the Rockers' Legacy Series

Sweet Agony

Book 2 of the Angels' Halo MC Next Gen Series

Made in the USA
Middletown, DE
04 November 2019

77996635R00161